W9-BUP-554

LOVE'S MASQUERADE

Marianne retreated from the mantelpiece to stand in front of the shelf of books. When Wolf followed, her breathing quickened. Why, when she was near him, couldn't she think clearly? And why did she always get so muddled whenever he spoke to her? This time, she vowed, she would hold her ground.

"You're not in Canada, Mr. Clinton," she said in her haughtiest tone. "You're in England now."

"More's the pity," Wolf said. He took a step forward and stood looking down at her, his blue eyes sparking dangerously. "In Canada we are very direct. When we know what we want, we go after it and take it."

Marianne felt a blush suffuse her face. "In Canada, in Canada, don't tell me again what they do in Canada!" she said.

"I won't," he replied. "I'll show you."

Wolf took her in his arms and drew her to him, his lips closing over hers in a tender, lingering kiss.

For an instant—only for an instant—she returned his kiss, then turned and fled from the library. She heard Wolf call after her, but she paid him no heed, listening only to the pounding of her heart, its beat seeming to warn her, over and over again, "Beware, beware, beware!"

THE BEST OF REGENCY ROMANCES

AN IMPROPER COMPANION (2691, $3.95)
by Karla Hocker
At the closing of Miss Venable's Seminary for Young Ladies school, mistress Kate Elliott welcomed the invitation to be Liza Ashcroft's chaperone for the Season at Bath. Little did she know that Miss Ashcroft's father, the handsome widower Damien Ashcroft would also enter her life. And not as a passive bystander or dutiful dad.

WAGER ON LOVE (2693, $2.95)
by Prudence Martin
Only a rogue like Nicholas Ruxart would choose a bride on the basis of a careless wager. And only a rakehell like Nicholas would then fall in love with his betrothed's grey-eyed sister! The cynical viscount had always thought one blushing miss would suit as well as another, but the unattainable Jane Sommers soon proved him wrong.

LOVE AND FOLLY (2715, $3.95)
by Sheila Simonson
To the dismay of her more sensible twin Margaret, Lady Jean proceeded to fall hopelessly in love with the silver-tongued, seditious poet, Owen Davies—and catapult her entire family into social ruin . . . Margaret was used to gentlemen falling in love with vivacious Jean rather than with her—even the handsome Johnny Dyott whom she secretly adored. And when Jean's foolishness led her into the arms of the notorious Owen Davies, Margaret knew she could count on Dyott to avert scandal. What she didn't know, however was that her sweet sensibility was exerting a charm all its own.

A Daring
Masquerade

Olivia Sumner

ZEBRA BOOKS
KENSINGTON PUBLISHING CORP.

ZEBRA BOOKS

are published by

Kensington Publishing Corp.
475 Park Avenue South
New York, NY 10016

First printing: November, 1991

Printed in the United States of America

Chapter One

"I'm all aflutter," Lucinda Beattie cried, staring raptly from the library window. "Lord Brandon's barouche is entering the square; now it's stopping in front of our town house; the footman is letting down the steps; he's opening the door. Oh, do come and look at Lord Brandon."

Old Mrs. Featheringill laid her book to one side. "I've seen Lord Brandon many, many times," she said, "just as I saw his father and *his* father before him."

"But not on such a day as this, not on the day Lord Brandon offers for Marianne." Lucinda drew in a sharp breath. "There he is, stepping down to the pavement dressed all in gray, a dark gray waistcoat, dove gray for the rest. He's so handsome he quite takes my breath away."

Mrs. Featheringill joined Lucinda at the window. "His father was just such a fine-looking man," she recalled, "until he yielded to the temptations of an over-abundant table."

"Lord Brandon's alone." Disappointment edged into Lucinda's voice. "Georgie's not with him."

"One doesn't bring a best friend when one intends to offer for a young lady's hand. At least they never did in my day." After watching Lord Brandon climb the steps to the Hilton town house, Mrs. Featheringill returned to her chair without further comment and picked up her book, *A True Account of the Balloon Crossing of the English Channel*.

"Georgie will surely be at the wedding," Lucinda said, turning from the window now that Lord Brandon was no longer in view. "What shall I wear to the announcement ball?" she asked. "We must have a ball, don't you agree, Mrs. F.; what would a London wedding be without a ball, especially now the war's over?"

Lucinda crossed the room to look up at her reflection in the glass above the fireplace. Tall and slender, with dark brown hair and hazel eyes, her appearance gave no hint of the industry and diligence with which she followed her chosen vocation. "Pink satin, I do believe," she said, "or perhaps lime. I was wearing green at our last musical evening when Georgie Stansbury complimented me on my gown. Which do you prefer, Mrs. Featheringill, pink or lime?"

The gray-haired woman looked up from her book. "I'd wait until the marriage contract is settled before choosing a gown," she advised.

"Do you mean you think there might not be a wedding after all? Surely you're funning me, Mrs. F. Isn't Lord Brandon the handsomest, the most elegant, the richest, the most eligible gentleman in all London? Didn't Wellington himself commend his ingenuity and valor at Waterloo? Isn't he a devotee of the arts and a sometimes thespian? Lord Brandon is the only man—with the possible exception of Georgie Stansbury—who quite exhausts my supply of superlatives."

"In my experience," Mrs. Featheringill pointed out tartly, "even the most eligible of gentlemen have been refused."

"Surely you don't consider Marianne to be addlepated. How could she refuse him? It's a perfect match, one made not here on earth but in heaven. And her grandfather could raise no objection to Lord Brandon."

"Alder Hilton would most certainly favor the match. In fact, he does favor it."

"There you are, then, the matter's settled. I'm so happy for Marianne; she deserves to make a good match after doing so much for me, rescuing me from the dreary fate of being a governess so that I'd have time to follow my muse. And she's done a great deal for others, yourself included, Mrs. F."

"All you say is true. You have, though, neglected to mention love. Isn't that a curious omission for someone who follows your vocation?"

"Love?" Lucinda was taken aback. "Lord Brandon's quite smitten with Marianne; his every glance proclaims his love. And how could she help but love him? I'll admit she's never *said* she loves Lord Brandon in so many words, but that's only because she's shy about expressing her innermost

7

thoughts. Yet I know for a fact she looks forward with eager anticipation to his visits, she enjoys the thrust and parry of his conversation, and she often quotes his *mots,* even those he's purloined from others. Especially those he's purloined."

Mrs. Featheringill pursed her mouth. "On the other hand, I've noticed her frown at some of his sallies. And at times she stares unseeingly at him."

Lucinda put a finger to her chin, puzzling over the other woman's words. *Could it be she sometimes thinks of the deaths of her mother and father?* she wondered. *I'd think, though, the passage of time should have healed her grief—after all, it happened many years ago.* A sound from the foyer drew Lucinda's attention. "At last," she said. "Lord Brandon is here."

She hurried to the doorway where, looking through the spray of water cascading from the fountain in the center of the foyer, she watched Lord Brandon follow Slater to the Hilton drawing room. John Cornwall, the fifth earl of Brandon, known to his friends as Brandon, was tall and fair, broad in the shoulders and erect, as befitted a former military officer.

"He makes *my* heart beat faster," Lucinda admitted, "and he's not the object of my affections nor I of his. Surely Marianne will accept him."

"We'll know soon enough." Mrs. Featheringill let her book fall to her lap, and she closed her eyes, her thoughts slipping away from the all-important meeting of Marianne and Lord Brandon. *Time will tell, as usual,* she thought. Letting her imagination roam free, she pictured herself ascending in the basket of a gaily colored balloon from the Dover cliffs, a brisk breeze carrying her toward France. . . .

Marianne paused in the drawing room doorway, her heart racing at the sight of Lord Brandon, who, unaware of her presence, stood with his back to her, his hands clasped behind him, frowning up at her grandfather Hilton's portrait over the chimneypiece. She savored the moment, smiling to herself as she fondly scrutinized him from the casual wave in his blond hair to the impeccable shine of his black shoes, remembering the very first time she had seen him. It had been at the Kier-Windom's, and he had been talking to Rolissa, frowning very much as he was now; and she recalled how even then, so many months ago, she had suspected and hoped the day would come when he would offer for her hand.

Today.

Their courtship was about to end and a new adventure to begin. Marianne felt an eagerness, a desire to put all uncertainties behind her—in the beginning wondering whether he cared and then later whether he cared as much as he claimed. Yet along with her hopefulness came an unease that pricked at her like a pin a dressmaker had forgotten to remove from a gown.

She remembered sitting beside her mother next to the fountain in the foyer long ago and hearing her mother sigh. "The year your father courted me," she said, "was the happiest year of my life. He was so handsome, so dashing, so charming, you can't imagine how all the other young women envied me!''

How wonderful, Marianne had thought at the time, *to marry for love, to be so happy.* Only later did she realize her mother had been telling her, without saying the actual words, that her life thereafter had been empty, lonely and drear.

Suddenly Lord Brandon straightened, and she knew he sensed, with that strange and marvelous intuition they seemed to have for one another's presence, that she was in the room. He turned with a smile, his blue eyes alight, and came to her, taking her hand and raising it to his lips, kissing her fingers tenderly. Her pulses raced, for no matter how many times it happened, her pleasant shock of excitement at his touch always took her by surprise.

"How lovely you look." He glanced in admiration at her black hair falling in ringlets framing her face, at her gown, his favorite, a cream silk with a frill at the bodice, at once simple, modest, and elegant.

Leading Marianne to the rose-patterned settee, Lord Brandon sat beside her. He pulled down his waistcoat, needlessly, and tightened the already tight knot of his cravat. How ill at ease he was! Was it possible that Lord Brandon, who had faced the French without flinching, could be daunted by a woman? By her?

Certainly his discomfiture didn't arise from his inexperience with the female sex. Hadn't his name been linked at one time or another with Rolissa and Rosemary, with Annabella and Anita, with Verity and Sophia, and many others? Only last month, tea table gossip had him strolling on the promenade in St. James's Park with Lillian Marsh.

Feeling compassion for him nonetheless— hadn't she been ill at ease many times herself?— Marianne broached an innocuous subject. "I imagine your aunt Jane is well on her way to Florence," she said.

He nodded. With relief, she thought. "I accompanied dear Aunt Jane to her ship yesterday morning," Lord Brandon said. "While I was at the Wapping docks, I was accidentally tripped up by an uncouth creature, a black-bearded Johnny Raw arriving from Canada on the *Queen of Ontario*. He was crowned by a dirty beaver cap and wore toggery fashioned from the untreated hides of animals.

"'Fare thee well, Wolf,' a sailor called down to him after I regained my feet, and in truth, the name fit him; he was a great hairy beast, more animal than man. As he was born to be. As he will continue to be for the remainder of his life. And, I'll wager, as he would rather be."

Marianne pictured the scene, the modish lord and the wolf man face to face, and she smiled, wondering what the new arrival must have thought of Lord Brandon in his finery. Did either of them wonder what it would be like to be in the other's place? She found it impossible to imagine Lord Brandon as a rustic. On the other hand, clean-shaven and properly attired, might not this

11

wolf man be taken for a lord? Providing, of course, he was careful not to speak. Yet language, and civilized manners as well, could be learned. . . .

"You're rather condescending," she told Lord Brandon.

"Am I?" He sounded puzzled. "I didn't intend to be; I only meant to say what I thought." When he smiled ruefully, she softened toward him as she always did. Why did she so enjoy goading Lord Brandon? Marianne wondered. Provoking quarrels was a game without a winner.

"I forgot," Lord Brandon went on, "that the Hilton clan has an affinity for the wilderness. Your grandfather shuns London to live in the highlands of Devon, and your father once planned to journey to America to recoup his fortune."

"And myself?" Marianne asked. "Do you think I secretly prefer noble savages to gentlemen of the ton?"

"No, but I'll warrant you might pretend to have such a preference merely to see if you could demolish my defense of those selfsame gentlemen of the ton."

"And what might your defense be?"

"I'd merely illustrate the merits of our English society by citing a few examples of gentlemen of my acquaintance who have distinguished themselves. Take Lord Garlington, for example. Does he have an equal as a patron of painting and music? Isn't his library the largest and most varied in all England?"

"I'll grant you that Lord Garlington is unsurpassed as a connoisseur. I wonder, though, if Lady

Garlington might prefer a less beneficent husband but one with fewer Other Connections."

Lord Brandon raised his eyebrows without commenting on what she'd said. "Another example," he told her, "is Lord Byron. What primitive red Indian from the plains or forests of North America could write such sublime poetry, could give pleasure to so many others?"

"And yet Lord Byron, for all his skill with words, resides not in London but in Venice, hounded from England by an outraged public. Lord Byron is constant only in his inconstancy. And don't tell me it's the way of our world, Lord Brandon. That it is bespeaks of the tragedy of our world."

"I hesitate to mention my good friend Brummel."

"And well you might, since only last year he fled to Calais to avoid paying his just debts."

Lord Brandon threw up his hands in mock surrender. "I should never attempt to joust with you, Miss Marianne; you always manage to vanquish me."

Looking at him with his arms raised, she felt a thrill of recognition. Who did he remind her of? A tingle coursed along her spine as she realized it was her father, dead these many years. Though Lord Brandon looked nothing like Terrence Hilton, he possessed the same easy good-humor, the charm, the joy in being alive that Hilton had exhibited.

How she had loved her father! It had been the steadfast and uncritical devotion of youth, she supposed, though no less ardent for that. Since she had seen him so infrequently, probably *because* she had seen him infrequently, their times together glowed in her memory as the happiest of her life—and this despite the terrible circumstances surrounding his death and all the heartbreak that followed.

"A penny," Lord Brandon said.

"The way you smiled and threw up your hands reminded me of my father."

"Thankfully of your father and not your grandfather. I wouldn't want to think I resembled old Alder." He raised his gaze to the portrait over the mantel. "Did I tell you that the last time I saw Alder he said, 'I expect you're tired of London by now, eh, Brandon?'"

Marianne smiled. "And I suppose you answered, 'Tired of London? When a man's tired of London, sir, he's tired of life.'"

"How did you guess?"

"Because that was Dr. Johnson's answer to the same question some forty years or more ago. According to Mrs. Featheringill, who knew him well."

"I might better have said, 'I may tire of life, my love for London may flag, but I'll never weary of your charming granddaughter.'"

Marianne smiled to acknowledge the compliment. Normally Lord Brandon's words would have delighted her, but the mention of her grandfather Alder cast a shadow over her pleasure. She loved the crusty old gentleman, yet he could be so stubborn, so unreasonable. His demands

14

brought forth the perverse in her.

"A few weeks ago, while I was waiting for you," Lord Brandon went on, "Mrs. Featheringill told me she had once expected Dr. Johnson, Dictionary Johnson, to ask her to marry him. This was when she was visiting Mrs. Thrale at Streatham. But he never brought himself to the point of posing the question."

"Did she tell you what her answer would have been?"

Lord Brandon shook his head.

"She intended to refuse him. 'I'll give you a bit of good advice,' she said to Lucinda and me. 'Whatever you do, never wed a man of genius unless you're seeking a lifetime of unhappiness.'"

"Marianne," Lord Brandon said, "I have a confession to make. For the past year, ever since I first met you at the Kier-Windom's, I've attempted to conceal the truth from you, but now you force my hand, and I must own to it."

"And what might that truth be, Lord Brandon?"

"I readily admit, despite what you may think, I'm not a man of genius, never was one, never will be one." He became serious. "Do you realize what that means?" he asked.

Marianne's heart skipped a beat. "Pray tell me what it means, Lord Brandon."

"I've tried so desperately to think of a new and clever way to make my declaration. I must have written a hundred protestations of affection only to throw each of them away as inadequate. I've searched the words of the poets, yes, Byron included, for phrases to use in praise of your beauty and charm, yet I've found none that do you justice."

He took her hand in his and looked intently into her eyes. "I've loved you from the very beginning," he told her, "even though at first I fought against my fate. Do you remember last November when I didn't call on you for a fortnight?"

"Only too well." How lonely she'd been, how perplexed and hurt by his sudden withdrawal.

"I wanted to break the spell you'd cast over me," Lord Brandon said. "I failed, I couldn't, I found it impossible to live without you. I love you, Marianne, love you with all my heart, and I want you for my wife."

"Brandon," she said, speaking low, her heart racing.

All at once she felt a flutter of panic. To quiet her agitation, she glanced away from him to the portrait of her grandfather, to the pair of perfume burners on the chimneypiece, to the flower-patterned fire screen. Why couldn't she meet his gaze?

"Are you all right?" he asked anxiously.

"I'm—I'm—" She hesitated before she went on. "I'm perfectly fine." At last she forced herself to look into his blue eyes, all the while shaking her head. "I can't marry you, Lord Brandon," she said, "I can't."

He sprang back as though she'd struck him. "You can't marry me? I don't understand. You've given me every reason to hope. Why in God's name can't you?"

"I can't." Marianne rose to her feet. "I can't, I just can't." Tears came to her eyes. What had she said? What was the matter with her? She loved him, didn't she? With a sob she turned from him and fled the room, leaving Lord Brandon staring after her in astonishment.

Chapter Two

Lord Brandon and George Stansbury drove off the stones and past the tollgate on their way to spend a weekend in the country visiting Harriet Ramsden at Litchfield Hall. Behind them a cloud of smoke and soot hung over London, but on both sides of George's new phaeton, birds sang their evensongs while ahead of them the last of the sunlight lingered on the rolling hills even as darkness gathered in the woods.

"The lemonade has failed me," Lord Brandon said. He sat holding his head in both hands.

"Prefer Dr. Ambrose's Tonic myself." George flicked his whip over the sorrel, hoping to arrive at his cousin's estate before dark.

Lord Brandon groaned as the horse increased its pace. "Your new phaeton jounces almost as much as your old one."

"Cost me a packet," George said. "Could afford it, though. Never had a better day at the races in my life. A triple, Brandon, a triple. Spanish Miss,

Crown's Gold, and Regal."

Lord Brandon nodded, understanding that his friend had wagered all his winnings from Spanish Miss on Crown's Gold and all those winnings on Regal.

"Tried to put my father onto Crown's Gold," George said. "Wouldn't listen to me."

"How is the general?" Lord Brandon asked.

"Just organized a new society." George smiled ruefully. "Calls it The Forlorn Female's Fund of Mercy or some such. Saving forlorn females and seeing me in the Army are his two goals in life."

"Being the only son of a wounded hero of Waterloo is your cross to bear."

"No matter what he did for father," George said, "I fear the Creator neglected to use a soldier's mold when he fashioned me."

George referred to his below average height, his stocky build, and his inclination to be both awkward and absent-minded. His saving grace was an all-encompassing friendliness proclaimed by his smile, and since he smiled often, that was what people remembered best about him.

"Not," George admitted, "that I've discovered the nature of the mold he did use."

"The mold of a boon companion, Georgie. I doubt there's any better."

For a time they rode in silence.

"The devil take Miss Marianne Hilton," Lord Brandon muttered as much to himself as to his friend. "The devil take all women while he's about it. There's nothing constant about them except their inconstancy."

"Well said, Brandon."

"The proper thing for me to do is climb to the parapet at Litchfield Hall and hurl myself to the flagstones below. What do you say, Georgie?"

George frowned, considering the question. "Don't think you should, all things considered. You'll never get the girl to marry you if you jump from Litchfield Tower."

"Perhaps I should hire a hot air balloon, ascend above London and leap from the basket."

"Cause a stir if you do, can't deny that. Never been done far as I know." George shook his head. "Can't predict who you might land on, got to think of that. And Miss Marianne, she wouldn't like it one bit. That girl would miss you something fierce, Brandon."

"Such would be my purpose, Georgie, to make her miss me."

"Instead of leaping to your death, you could go down to Brighton. Or to Bath. Or Paris, for that matter. If you did, you could always come back to London when you grew bored, got to think of that."

"If I traveled abroad, Marianne might not miss me at all. She'd be certain to miss me if I could never return."

"Brandon, *I'd* miss you awfully, either way. By more than half."

"Damn it, Georgie, I'm not about to leap from either a balloon or a tower; where's the challenge in that? I intend to marry the girl." Lord Brandon sighed. "I love her, Georgie, and I need her. My heart leaps every time I set eyes on her; I can't sleep nights for thinking of her. Damme if I can fathom her objections. Does she think me inconstant? Frivolous? A gamester who'll one day be imprisoned for debt? Does she consider me a four-bottle man? Whatever her reason, there must be something I can do to change her mind, but confound it all, I don't know what."

"Good thing she didn't see you last night. Only two bottles, though, not four."

"I don't know what you're talking about, Georgie."

"You were awfully foxed, Brandon, that's what. I'll wager you don't remember what happened."

"I recall the entire evening perfectly. I wanted to forget Marianne, so you and I went to the Cocoa Tree, where we met Chichester and the others. And I was *not* foxed."

"Then, you must recall the footrace."

"The footrace? Last night?" Lord Brandon frowned. "Let me think. Yes, I do remember Chi boasting of his prowess as a runner. So I challenged him to a three-mile race on the Oxford Road. You see, Georgie, my memory of last evening is flawless."

"Nothing a bit peculiar about the race, Brandon? A bit out of the way?"

"Peculiar? Don't talk in riddles."

"The notion of racing the three miles by running backward was yours, Brandon; you do grant me that, don't you?"

"Backward?" Lord Brandon slapped his thigh. "Of course, that jogs my memory. Running

22

backward. Without the handicap, I'd have out-distanced Chi by half a mile or more." Lord Brandon rubbed his nape. "Georgie, is that how I came by this stiff neck?"

George nodded. "You might not have won," he said, "if Chi hadn't fallen over the goose and bruised his leg."

"I don't need the help of geese to outrun Chichester, forward or backward."

George flicked the reins. "Fitting, Chi said, you being the one to propose a backward race. Maintained you prefer doing most things backward."

"You don't agree with Chi, do you, Georgie?"

"Have to admit you don't always look ahead. Don't always see where your notions are apt to lead you."

"I'll let you in on a secret, Georgie. Last month while at Scarborough hall, I practiced running backward in the event Chichester ever suggested a footrace. Anyone can run forward; it takes a man of special vision to run backward. And win. I become bored with the commonplace."

"Perhaps Marianne prefers the humdrum. Can't see any other reason for her to turn you down."

"That's part of the puzzle, Georgie. For a woman, she has a keen sense of adventure. The whole affair perplexes me."

"Girl doesn't appreciate you, Brandon. Reads too many novels, expects someday a knight will ride up to her town house and carry her off to his castle in Scotland. Lancelot, Galahad, one of those chaps. She's not worth your time, Brandon. Let the devil take her."

Lord Brandon stiffened. "Take that back, Georgie," he demanded.

"But you yourself said—"

"I can ask the devil to take Miss Marianne. You can't."

"Pray accept my humblest apology, Lord Brandon. Hope the devil doesn't take her." George, disliking any unpleasantness, changed the subject. "Happen to talk to Miss Lucinda?" he asked.

"I thought I spied her gazing down at me from a window when I arrived," Lord Brandon said. "Didn't see her after that. Probably at work fashioning the latest of her romantic tales."

"Read a few pages to me," George said. *The Ramsden Curse*, she calls it."

"Heaven protect us from female scribblers. Lucinda's undoubtedly put the prospect of impossible romantic bliss into Marianne's head with stories of rugged Scottish lairds and noble Indian chieftains."

"Dash it all," George protested, "there are worse things women can do than scribble."

Lord Brandon extended his forefinger. "One comes to mind." He extended a second finger. "No, perhaps two."

"Two?" George asked, interested. "What's the second?"

"I hate to see a woman who's too fond of spirits."

"That's a proclivity, Brandon, not an occupation."

"A near thing, either way." Lord Brandon kneaded his forehead with his gloved fingers. "I think Miss Lucinda fancies you, Georgie," he said.

George reddened.

Lord Brandon stared at him for a moment in surprise, then raised his hands as though to comment, *Wonders will never cease.* All at once he pointed ahead of them. "Look there, Georgie, a horseman reined in at Tart's Turn."

The rider, silhouetted against the crimson-streaked sky, had stopped at the spot where the road from London to Litchfield veered sharply to the right. Oblivious to their approach, he stared across the fields at the dark outline of the great Hall.

"Don't recognize the blighter," George said. "From the way he sits his horse and by the general look of him, I would have said it was you, Brandon, if I didn't know you were right here next to me. Not a local, know all the locals. Better see what he's about; Cousin Harriet's all alone at the Hall."

"You can hardly maintain she's alone," Lord Brandon objected, "when she has a staff of twenty-five."

"Same as being alone." George slowed the phaeton and reined up beside the rider.

The man gave a start as though roused from a deep reverie. When he turned to face them, Lord Brandon found himself staring at a black-bearded stranger in a dark many-caped riding coat and a high black hat. He'd seen the young man before; he'd swear to it. By God, it was the Canadian from the docks. What was his name?

"Wolfson Clinton," the stranger told them in answer to George's introductions.

"Riding to the Hall?" George asked. "We're bound there; we'll ride with you."

Wolf Clinton shook his head. "Wanted a look at the place, no more," he said. "Must have heard of it back home in Canada when I was a young'un. Always dreamed of someday seeing Litchfield Hall. Beautiful old pile, ain't she?"

"We're staying at the Hall for a few days," George said, his generous nature coming to the fore. "Ride there with us, have a bite and share a bottle, glad to show you around, the maze and all. My cousin's, you know, on my mother's side."

Again Wolf shook his head. "Thank you, sir, but I have no time to spare. Shouldn't have ridden here at all except I had to see the Hall. I sail tomorrow for Calais and then travel on to Paris."

"The invitation stands on your return," George said.

"Might never come back to England. My business is contracting with warehousemen and merchants to import Canadian furs, and I hope for greater enthusiasm on the Continent than I've found here." He touched the brim of his hat in a salute. "Good night and godspeed to you gentlemen." With a last glance at the Hall, Wolf swung his horse in the direction of London and was quickly lost to sight in the gathering gloom.

"Strange coincidence," Lord Brandon said as

they rode on toward the Hall. "I literally fell over that fellow, that Wolfson Clinton, after he disembarked from the *Queen of Ontario*. Matter of fact, I told Marianne about him. She seemed quite taken with the idea of a Canadian from the wilds of North America."

"Well-spoken chap," George said. "For a colonial."

Lord Brandon went on as though George hadn't said a word. "At times I can almost read Marianne's mind. I've been able to surprise her more than once." He smiled. "I suspect she was intrigued by that wilderness man being so different from me. Since she refused me, perhaps my opposite would appeal to her."

"Looked a bit like you, Brandon. Without the beard, with his clothes brought up to snuff, and with fair hair, I might mistake him for you. At a distance."

"Noble savages!" Lord Brandon snorted. "They're actually dirty brutes, every last one of them. Women harbor the most peculiar ideas. If they ever met one face to face, they'd change their opinions quick enough."

"Leave a woman stranded with wild heathens for a time," George said, "she'd soon tire of them. Like Robinson Crusoe, she'd be building bonfires of driftwood and tying her shawl to trees trying to be rescued."

"Georgie!" Lord Brandon clapped his friend on the shoulder. "That's it, by Jove, that's what I'll do. You've given me a glorious notion."

"Maroon Miss Marianne on a desert island? Bit

of an undertaking, that." He pondered the problem. "Nearest barren island's probably in Scotland, have to hire a ship. Need a crew. Might fly there in that hot air balloon."

"No, no, Georgie, I don't intend to strand Marianne on a desert island. More like bringing the island here."

"To London? Even more of a chore, that. Couldn't use the balloon, for starters. Have to—"

"I don't intend to transport an entire island here, merely one of its natives. Not just any native, a particular one. Mr. Wolfson Clinton as a matter of fact. And no, Georgie, not Mr. Clinton in the flesh, an impersonator of that gentleman, an impostor, an impostor who will look like Mr. Clinton, speak like Mr. Clinton, behave in every way like Mr. Clinton, and yet not be Mr. Clinton. An impostor who will be none other than myself."

"Don't know, Brandon. Rather a hum, that. Marianne might not like it."

"She'll never know. Once she learns how wrongheaded she's been, once she comes to appreciate Lord Brandon, Mr. Clinton will disappear, never to be seen again."

"Brandon, only you could have thought of such a coil. You can bring it off, too. Amateur theatricals. You played Othello, didn't you? At Oxford."

"Othello's more in Clinton's line. I played Hamlet, Prince of Denmark."

"I remember. 'Good night, sweet Prince.' And you *do* resemble Clinton."

"With the unwitting help of your cousin

28

Harriet, I'll arrange an introduction to Marianne, behaving in a harmless fashion at our first meeting. Only later, Georgie, will I reveal friend Clinton's true colors, have him behave like the brute he undoubtedly is, so Marianne will come flying into my arms. Into Lord Brandon's arms, that is."

"You'll not upset the poor girl, will you, Brandon? I wouldn't want her harmed."

"Of course I won't harm her. Don't I love Marianne? I'm doing this for her own good. I'll merely insult her, show her the underlying bestial nature of mankind. All mankind with the exception of Lord Brandon, who, in comforting her, will prove to be every inch the understanding gentleman."

George slowed to turn in between the stone pillars at the entrance to Litchfield Hall, the dirt driveway winding in front of them into a copse where the lights of the main building flickered through the trees. Overhead the evening star shone like a sentinal in the west; the once crimson clouds on the horizon had darkened. The May air was cool and invigorating with the fresh scents of the earth's rebirth pervading the night.

It was an evening to encourage young men to believe all things were possible.

"Just recalled," George said, "Marianne visits Litchfield Hall in a week's time."

"Good, that's when I'll arrange to meet her, then."

"Have to concoct a story, Brandon. Wolf Clinton's history. Why he's in London and all."

"In any deception, you must hew as close to the truth as possible. I'll be a seller of wild animal pelts who's journeyed to London to encourage trade with my Canadian company. I'll require a reason for knowing your cousin Harriet." He stared ahead at the dark bulk of the Hall as though seeking inspiration. "Wasn't there a guide leading the tragic journey in Canada when Harriet's husband and son were drowned? Since this Wolf Clinton is about my age, twenty-five give or take a few years, I'll make him the son of the guide. He's traveled here on business as well as to pay his respects to the wife of his father's friend and former employer."

George shook his head vehemently. "Won't do at all. Not fair to Harriet, not in the least. Bring back old memories best left buried. Remind her of her son's tragic death and all. Can't do that to her, Brandon." He paused and added, "Sorry."

"Your point's well taken. Perhaps Wolf's father knew Lord Litchfield, always admired the earl, the elder Clinton's now dead and his lawyer gave the son letters of introduction. Would Harriet help Clinton under those conditions? I don't want to reveal my true identity to her. The fewer people who know a secret, the better."

"Certain she would. Might help even if she knew of your scheme. Harriet's close to Marianne, close as she gets to anyone. Thinks you ought to marry Marianne, Brandon, claims you're a ship without a rudder."

"And your cousin Harriet is a ship without a captain. She hasn't been seen in society since Lord

Litchfield was killed fourteen years ago. If she's not careful, she'll end up a recluse."

"What if Marianne recognizes you?" George asked, ever eager to avoid argument.

"She won't. I'll have my hair dyed, purchase a full beard from an actor's providing shop near the Covent Garden and wear nondescript clothes."

"'The apparel oft proclaims the man.' That's Hamlet, Brandon."

"I know. Good God, Georgie, it's only been four years since I trod the boards. I can't spout Shakespeare when I'm Clinton, though; I'll have to talk like a Canadian."

"Do you know how Canadians talk?" George asked, interested.

"No, but neither does Marianne. I'll have to buy chewing tobacco, too, and give up snuff for a few days." His eyes gleamed. "A challenge, Georgie, this will be the greatest challenge of my life."

"But if she *does* recognize you?"

"I'll tell her my impersonation of Clinton was the result of a wager. Women believe men at their clubs wager on everything and anything. A wager made with you, Georgie, or with Chichester."

"If anyone can bring it off, you can, Brandon."

"From now on," Lord Brandon said, "call me Wolf."

Chapter Three

"Are you still feeling poorly?" Lucinda asked. "Is there anything I can get you? Would you like a nice cup of hot tea?"

Marianne shook her head vigorously. "Thank you, no. I'm fine, perfectly fine, a touch of the megrims, nothing more."

"I'll be happy to ride to Harriet's with you this morning. I have nothing planned, so if you'd enjoy having company, I can be ready to leave in a few minutes."

"No, no, you must stay here in London and finish your book; you've fallen behind as it is."

Why must Lucinda treat her as an invalid to be waited on and pampered merely because Lord Brandon hadn't called or written in the ten days since she refused him? She could get along perfectly well without Brandon. By keeping busy she didn't think about him. At least not all of the time.

She had so many things to do. Today she'd visit

Harriet Ramsden at Litchfield Hall. And weren't she and Lucinda attending the theater next week with General and George Stansbury? And hadn't she and Lucinda planned a musical evening for later in the month? And she really should visit Grandfather Hilton at Edgemoor soon. She'd been postponing the trip to Devon since before Easter.

Yes, so much to do, so many people to call on, so many obligations to fulfill. Why then did the clatter of a carriage in the square make her heart flutter? Why did she eagerly await the arrival of the post? Why, without Brandon, did the days, weeks and months stretch endlessly ahead of her like an indistinct track across a desert?

"Would you listen to a page from *The Ramsden Curse* before you leave?" Lucinda asked. "I've just written the section on the fate of poor Frederic."

"I'd love to hear it." Didn't she have books to read, games of whist to play, shopping to do? She wasn't like Harriet Ramsden; she didn't intend to become a recluse.

Lucinda rearranged the sheets of paper on the drawing room table before looking up at Marianne. "As I told you," she said, "by the time I submit my manuscript to Trotter and Sons, I'll have changed all the real names to fictitious ones. Using the names of actual people like the Ramsdens makes the writing so much easier when I do my first drafts."

"Harriet can hardly object to that. All the same, it's best we don't mention your method of first drafts to her just in case it might upset her."

Marianne closed her eyes and settled back in her chair.

Lucinda nodded her agreement. "This fragment begins," she said, "after Frederic's brother is tragically killed in a riding accident. His father is so grief-stricken by his son's death, he goes into seclusion for six months."

"Of course, Harriet only had the one son, only Frederic," Marianne pointed out, opening her eyes.

"I added a brother to make the story more dramatic. And to give Edward a more compelling reason for traveling to Canada." Lucinda cleared her throat. "At the end of the sixth month," she read, "Edward Ramsden, Earl of Litchfield, emerged from seclusion to announce a startling scheme.

"He proposed to accept a mission for his government and, leaving his estate in the care of his wife, Harriet, sail to Canada. The harsh and challenging surroundings of a new world would, he believed, assuage his own grief while giving his ten-year-old son the advantages of a rugged life in order to cure him of his sickliness and, hopefully, of his mathematical inclinations as well.

" 'If worse comes to worst, by God,' the earl told Harriet, 'Frederic may at least discover new equations for his wretched mathematical problems and new rhymes for his couplets.'

"Five months later, a letter from the earl's recently retained solicitors in Montreal brought the unwelcome word that the earl and little

Frederic were two weeks tardy in returning from a journey into the interior.

"Apprehension shivered through Litchfield Hall; Harriet became distraught. A groom met each succeeding post in the village, and his return to the Hall was awaited with a mixture of foreboding and hope. Finally the feared calamity was confirmed. The earl and Frederic, canoeing on the St. Maurice with a Canadian guide, were negotiating a rapids when the canoe capsized. The earl drowned, and his son was swept away.

"Their guide, after regaining consciousness, buried the earl in a forest glade and then led the unsuccessful search for some trace of Frederic. There was no chance the younger Ramsden had survived, the guide reported to the mourning family in England."

Lucinda finished reading, sat back in her chair and looked questioningly at Marianne.

"Bravo Lucinda!" Marianne cried. "I can't think of any improvements. You make the gothic tale of the Ramsdens clear and compelling."

"I'd prefer, when I write my next book, God willing, to describe less tragic events. The romance of your mother and father, for instance, between Terrence Hilton and Elizabeth Royce, their courtship and eventual marriage over the opposition of his father, Alder, their life together, their travels, the young couple's plan to emigrate to America, and finally your father's death in a duel while defending your mother's honor. Not using their real names, of course."

Marianne rose abruptly and walked to the

drawing room window. "You make their life together sound romantic, yet I suspect it wasn't really that way at all. My mother and father's story wouldn't make engaging fiction."

Not the true story, at least. Why had her mother lied? Marianne asked herself. Why hadn't she ever revealed the actual circumstances of her father's death? Perhaps now, after all these years, it no longer mattered. Perhaps—

"My lady." She turned from the window at the sound of Slater's voice. "Your carriage awaits," he said from the doorway.

"In a few minutes." She watched Slater bow and leave the room.

"I'll certainly abide by your wishes," Lucinda promised. "I never realized you might object."

"The past is best left undisturbed," Marianne told her. All of the past, the tragedy of her mother and father and, more recently, her refusal of Lord Brandon. What was done was done.

Shortly after noon Marianne rode in her new landau between the stone pillars and onto the winding drive leading to Litchfield Hall. The May sun shone warmly into the open carriage, but in the west, thunderheads threatened rain before nightfall.

Having vowed not to think of Lord Brandon, she discovered she could think of little else. In all likelihood, she told herself, he'd repaired to a spa or a race meeting to heal his bruised spirits by wagering, carousing, and pursuing bits of muslin or whatever *chere-amies* were styled this season. Perhaps by now he'd forgotten her completely.

Her coachman lowered the steps and swung open the door of the landau, jolting Marianne into an awareness that she had arrived at Litchfield Hall.

Leaving the carriage, she climbed one of the pair of curving stairways to the entrance porch on the second level. The Hall, elegant and Italianate, a great stone structure built in the 1730's by the architect William Adam, featured a central building three stories tall and two wings of two stories gracefully linked to the main hall by curving colonnades of arches. Above the gently sloping roofs rose the chimneys, a proliferation of chimneys.

"Lady Litchfield is expecting you," Chilton informed Marianne as he led her through the central hallway to the rear portico. "She hopes you'll join her in the herb garden."

Marianne paused at the top of the steps leading down to the garden to raise her parasol. Harriet Ramsden, her back to the house, sat beneath a pale blue sunshade on a white, metal grillwork chair staring across the lawns at a long hedge of lilacs. The sweet scent of the flowers mingled with the more pungent odors of the herbs.

With her graying chestnut hair drawn severely back into an unfashionable bun, Harriet appeared ten years older than her forty-four years. Her green gown, dowdy and out-of-date, made Marianne's sedate blue walking dress seem chic in comparison.

Marianne descended the stone steps, hoping the sound of her approach would alert the older woman to her presence. When Harriet gave no sign she heard her, Marianne asked, "Aren't the lilacs lovely this year?"

Harriet gave a start of surprise, turned, then rose and ran to Marianne, clasping her in her arms. Stepping back, she looked up at her visitor with uncertain green eyes. "We'll stroll in the maze today?" Harriet often put her suggestions in the form of questions.

"Of course," Marianne agreed. Though Harriet seemed the most tentative of women, Marianne knew she held strong opinions which she seldom hesitated to express. Since Harriet had long admired Lord Brandon, Marianne was prepared to be chided for refusing him.

"The most extraordinary thing happened to me yesterday," Harriet said, "in Edward's office in the west wing. I was reading his journal describing his tour of Canada when suddenly a great flapping and screeching came from the very walls of the room. What could it be? I asked myself. Surely not ghosts in the middle of the afternoon?

"I summoned Harris at once, and he soon found the source of the uproar. Birds were culprits, swifts trapped in one of the chimneys by falling bricks. Harris had the most dreadful time rescuing them because they wanted to fly upward when their only escape was down through the fireplace. How obstinate they were! Harris finally forced them into Edward's office, and we shooed them out the window."

"The poor birds," Marianne said.

"Yet their predicament was mostly their own fault? They were so accustomed by habit to flying skyward, they couldn't bring themselves to go any other way. Even to save their lives."

The two women left the garden and entered the Litchfield labyrinth where the walls of yew, that ancient symbol of grief, stood six feet high on both sides of them, muting sounds from the outside world. Above the hedges, mountains of dark clouds rose into a cobalt sky.

"I'm like those swifts." Harriet's words came in a rush. "Trapped in a life of habit."

Marianne, surprised at Harriet's view of herself, started to object, to deny the truth of what the other woman had said, but decided to remain silent. Harriet *was* akin to those birds in the wall.

"If I'm the swifts and the bricks are life's inevitable decay," Harriet went on, "I suppose the chimney is Litchfield Hall. I wonder who Harris is; who will come to rescue me? Or whether anyone will."

"We have to find our own way for the most part," Marianne said, "whether escaping from habit or keeping to the right path in mazes like this one."

The alleys between the almost impenetrable evergreen hedges led, Marianne knew, in a series of zigzags past numerous enticing dead ends to an open center where a stone bench faced a pedestal surmounted by a sundial and one of the few moondials in existence. Though the key to arriving at the center was well known—right, left,

left, and then always right—even Harriet Ramsden at times became lost in the intricate convolutions of the alleyways.

Lord Byron had visited his friend Edward Ramsden at the Hall many times, and when the poet had written that Childe Harold "through Sin's long labyrinth had run," it was widely believed the phrase had been inspired by the Litchfield labyrinth.

"Lord Brandon and my cousin George Stansbury stayed at the Hall last week," Harriet said as they turned left for the second time. "Poor Brandon was suffering from an acute case of the dismals, so after he left, he told me, he intended to travel on to Bath."

Marianne, suspecting she was about to be blamed for those dismals, said nothing.

"I understand why you refused him," Harriet said. "In many ways Lord Brandon's heedlessness and his inconstancy remind me of my Edward at that age."

Marianne stopped for a moment, for she was surprised, no, more than surprised, startled at Harriet's mention of Edward and Lord Brandon in the same breath. She had always believed that, in Harriet's mind, Edward Ramsden was incomparable.

"When I met Edward," Harriet went on, "he was a dashing blade who'd left many a broken heart strewn in his romantic wake. After we married, he changed, of course, but there's no assurance Lord Brandon will have the necessary strength of character to do the same."

"I don't think he's *that* set in his ways," Marianne argued.

"He does have the advantage of great wealth," Harriet said, "but I know you don't set a high value on that."

"My grandfather Alder does; I don't. On the other hand, I don't fault Lord Brandon for being wealthy. He's what he was born to be, a gentleman of the ton."

"Yes," Harriet agreed, "but what are gentlemen of the ton these days? For the most part they prefer dissipation to sobriety, inconstancy to faithfulness, wagering on dice, cards, and horses to the practice of thrift. At the moment they all see themselves as cocks of the walk. I often wonder where these selfsame gentleman will be ten years hence. Dead? In exile? In Marsalsea or some other debtor's prison?"

"Lord Brandon's not like that!" Marianne protested. She frowned. Why was she defending him so vehemently? she wondered. Was she being perverse or were her feelings about Lord Brandon really more confused than she was prepared to admit?

"Well, I never said he was, did I?" Harriet smiled. "Regardless of Lord Brandon's merits or lack thereof, other eligible gentlemen reside in London. My cousin George, for one, is difficult to dislike."

"Lucinda's quite taken with Georgie, though most of the time I'm not certain he knows she exists. He is engaging, no one can deny that, yet I wish he didn't take everything one says so literally.

Too often he understands one's words perfectly and the meaning not at all."

"A fault of many of us?" After Harriet led Marianne around the final turning, they sat side by side on the stone bench at the heart of the labyrinth. "I've known the Hilton family for many years," Harriet said. "Do you know which one you most remind me of?"

Marianne considered. "My mother?"

"You have your mother's comeliness, blue eyes and raven hair and a touch of your father's restless ways. Yet more than anyone you bring to mind your grandfather. Alder Hilton."

Marianne, taken aback, glanced quickly at Harriet and realized she was in earnest. Alder Hilton, that unbending, reclusive, tyrannical patriarch. She certainly didn't resemble him! "No, not Grandfather Alder," she protested.

"I do believe he left London to live at Edgemoor after his son's death because everyone urged him not to go. He's an obstinate man? I wouldn't describe you as obstinate, Marianne, you're too young. Stubborn, perhaps, is a better word?"

Not wanting to quarrel with her friend, she didn't reply, and Harriet, too, was silent. Lowering her parasol, Marianne let the afternoon sun warm her face while she watched a gold and black butterfly flutter aimlessly to and fro between the hedges as though lost in the maze. The butterfly finally alighted on the arm of the moondial.

She might be stubborn, Marianne admitted to herself, but in no other way did she resemble her grandfather. Not that she wasn't fond of the old gentleman, she was; she also felt sorry for him. She recalled the last time she visited him at Edgemoor when, on the final day of her stay, her grandfather, limping from the gout, had walked with her to the stone tower on a rise overlooking the moors. The October day had been gray, though all the days she spent at Edgemoor, no matter the weather, seemed gray to Marianne.

Standing in the lookout at the top of the tower, Alder Hilton pointed with his cane to Edgemoor House, built a hundred years before by his grandfather. "At first there was but the house," he told her, "surrounded by a few tillable acres." he swung his cane in a circle. "Now all this is Hilton land," he said with pride.

Marianne nodded, dreading what was coming, knowing her grandfather's message almost by heart. She tried to shut both her ears and her mind, but still some of his words stabbed through to jab at her like thorns: "We're the last of the Hiltons, you and I . . . a grandchild, if only I had a grandchild . . . a boy or a girl, it matters not . . . an heir of good blood and breeding . . . Lord Brandon . . ."

At the mention of Brandon's name, she roused from her withdrawal to give him her full attention.

"I approve of Lord Brandon," her grandfather said. "A good family, the Cornwalls. You can judge the quality of the horse by its stable."

44

"I hardly know the gentleman." At the time this was true, more or less.

He eyed her closely before saying, "I don't begrudge you the expense of your establishment in London. I am, however, a man who has always expected to receive good value for his money."

Her anger flared. She wasn't an investment in two percents; she was his granddaughter. "Any time you want me to move here to care for you," she said, "you have only to say the word."

"You've inherited your father's temper." Alder looked down from the tower at the bleak expanse of the moors. "I recall the day young Terry was thrown and had to walk some five miles home. Even now I can hear him storming into the house—" Her grandfather's voice faltered, and he looked away from her as he stifled a sob.

Marianne went to him and put her arms around him, tears filling her eyes. When he turned to her, she thought he was about to take her into his arms and let her comfort him, but instead he pushed her away, descended the circular stair and strode, limping, across the moor, leaving her to follow far behind. . . .

The butterfly on the moondial suddenly took flight, fluttering higher and higher until it was lost to her sight. A strange stillness enveloped the two women in the labyrinth, a complete quiet, as if the Earth had paused for the space of a heartbeat or two.

The hairs on Marianne's nape rose.

Something was watching. *Someone.* Watching *her*. She was certain of it. Her pulses raced; her hand closed on Harriet's wrist. There! A stranger stood on the portico at the rear of Litchfield Hall, his hands on the stone balustrade, staring down into the labyrinth. At them. No, at her.

She didn't recognize him. Or did she? He seemed so familiar. Where had she seen that black beard, tailed fur cap, and fringed buckskin garb before? No, of course she'd never seen him, but she'd heard of him. He was the Canadian described by Lord Brandon.

The wolf man.

Chapter Four

Marianne stared at the stranger, fascinated in spite of herself. He was exactly as Lord Brandon had described him, a hairy creature from another world, a savage transplanted from the wilds of America to civilized England. What in the name of heaven had brought him to Litchfield Hall?

Evidently he'd acquired little or no patina of civilization on his long journey from his homeland. Perhaps he didn't want to change; perhaps he was satisfied with what he was. Could that be possible? She shook her head. Everyone possessed the impulse to improve, Marianne believed, to make themselves better than they were.

This wolf man would be no exception.

He was staring back at her. As if she, Marianne Hilton, were the exhibit in a menagerie. From this distance she wasn't able to read his expression. Even at close range only his eyes might yield a clue to his thoughts, for his shaggy black beard effectively concealed the rest of his face.

A tremor coursed through her—curiosity? fear? a premonition? some unknown and unacknowledged emotion?—causing her to look hastily away. She decided she didn't want to know what thoughts lurked in his mind after all.

"What is it?" Harriet asked. "You look to be in a bit of a quake."

"On the portico. That stranger."

Harriet rose so that she could peer over the hedges, her mouth opening slightly in surprise when she spied the man in buckskin looking down at them.

"When will these colonials learn manners?" Harriet gave an exaggerated shake of her head. "They're so audacious, you'd think they'd never heard of leaving their cards or writing letters to make appointments for interviews. They have the oddest notion that the way to talk to someone is to simply arrive and begin conversing."

Still perturbed, Marianne could only echo Harriet's words. "He's a colonial?"

"A Canadian? He arrived on the *Queen of Ontario* a fortnight ago bearing letters of introduction from a Montreal solicitor to Smead and Callahan. They're my solicitors? He inquired after us, the Ramsdens and Litchfield Hall. His name is Mr. Clinton, Mr. Wolfson Clinton. Wolfson! Did you ever hear of such a bizarre name in your life?"

"It sounds invented. Or perhaps it's a family name."

"Come up to the Hall with me, Marianne. I may as well dispose of whatever business Mr. Clinton

48

has with me. If I don't, he'll only return again and again until I do."

Marianne drew back without knowing why. "If you don't mind, I'd rather stay here."

"We may have a storm?" Threatening thunderheads now darkened more than half the sky.

"I'll join you later, Harriet. Mr. Clinton's visit has nothing to do with me. I've found my way out of this maze many a time."

With a last questioning look, Harriet, promising to hurry back, left Marianne in the center of the labyrinth. When Marianne glanced again at the portico, Wolf Clinton was no longer there.

She sat on the stone bench, her mind in a turmoil. Why was she so reluctant to meet the man? Because his uncouthness repelled her? No, she had to be truthful; she prided herself on her honesty. Quite the opposite was the case. Some aspect of him actually appealed to her.

Certainly not his appearance or the rude way he'd stared down at her. What was it, then? She blinked as the revelation burst into her mind. He was a challenge. She'd mentioned to Lord Brandon her belief the wolf man could be transformed into an English gentleman. Could *she* make him over? Now that she'd seen him, the task seemed formidable. It was also true that men weren't Punches to be guided by an unseen hand. If she suggested any such scheme to him, he'd think her mad. Everyone would. Yet the idea tempted her nonetheless.

Hearing thunder rumble in the west, Marianne

began walking slowly along the alleyway leading from the labyrinth's heart. When Harriet had first explored the maze years before, she had told Marianne, it was the custom to take a ball of yarn—a clue—along to unwind so as to leave an easy trail to follow back to the entrance. Once you learned the way, the clues were no longer necessary.

If only, Marianne thought, she could leave a trail of clues to help her find her way out of life's labyrinths. It would be to no avail, of course. Life wasn't the same as a maze, since in life you couldn't go into the past and start anew no matter how hard you tried.

Marianne stopped short. She frowned, finding herself in a cul-de-sac with hedges on three sides blocking her path. With all her musing, she'd made a wrong turning. She retraced her steps and at the first juncture pondered before deciding to go to the left. Again she found herself in a cul-de-sac.

Thunder reverberated around the Hall. Once more she hurried back the way she'd come and turned in the other direction. Again she found her path blocked by yew hedges. A frisson of panic surprised her. She hurried in the opposite direction, her pace quickening. She turned right, almost running now, holding her blue skirt in one hand, turned right again, her pulses racing, turned left.

Good, she saw a long alleyway ahead of her. She began to slow, to breathe easier, confident she'd found the way to the entrance.

The alley ended in a wall of yew. How could she have gone wrong? She swung around and ran, turned, turned again, then thought she heard a voice calling her name. Harriet's voice? She rushed forward, rounded another corner and stopped, a cry of fright on her lips.

Wolf Clinton loomed in front of her, his arms reaching for her.

Marianne sprang back in alarm.

Making no attempt to approach her, Wolf Clinton raised his hands, palms toward her, in what she understood to be a gesture—in red Indian sign language?—showing he meant her no harm. His hands, she noted, were clad in new and fashionable chicken-skin gloves.

He muttered a few words in such a deep and throaty voice Marianne didn't comprehend his meaning at first, though his tone seemed to be friendly. She drew in several breaths to quell her fear. As he went on talking, his meaning gradually became clear. Evidently he had wished only to stop her from running into him and harming herself.

Wolf's left hand fell to his side, and he extended his right. Puzzled, she looked at the gloved hand, wondering whether he meant to take her hand in his and raise it to his lips or whether he wanted her to shake hands with him. Her heart beating wildly, unable to move, she stared at his proferred hand until he drew it back.

"Marianne, I was so worried."

Startled, she looked past Wolf and saw Harriet hurrying toward them along the alleyway. "I'm so glad," Harriet said breathlessly when she joined them. "Mr. Clinton has found you safe and sound?"

Marianne nodded, uncomfortably aware of Wolf Clinton's steady gaze. "I'm perfectly fine," she said, avoiding Wolf's intent blue eyes, angry with herself because of her moment of unreasoning fear, even more upset because she'd let this stranger be aware of that fear.

"I feel a drop of rain?" Harriet said. "We must all hasten back to the Hall before we're drenched. Oh, I'm sorry. Miss Marianne Hilton, may I present Mr. Wolfson Clinton, recently of Montreal, Canada."

With the briefest nod of acknowledgement, Marianne hastened past Wolf and followed Harriet along the alleyway. Again she noticed Wolf's fine vellum gloves, puzzling over them, wondering if he had started outfitting himself in a civilized manner on his arrival in London only to abandon the effort immediately after buying the gloves.

When Wolf followed her toward the exit from the maze, she saw from the corner of her eye that the Canadian walked with a slight limp, favoring his right leg.

"A bar," Wolf said to her in his husky voice. A brandy voice, Grandfather Alder would have labeled it, the result of years of over-indulgence, one of the least pernicious effects of being a six-bottle man.

Really, this Mr. Wolfson Clinton was proving

to be impossible. To add to her distress, she had no idea what he was trying to tell her.

"A bar, Mr. Clinton?" she asked.

"A bar." He slapped his right thigh.

How crude he was! She was thankful to see Harris on the portico keeping a watchful eye on their progress. Evidently Mr. Wolfson Clinton had been injured in a melee of some sort, what some called a punchup.

"You were struck by a bar?" she asked.

"Yup, a grizzly bar."

"A gray bar? You mean an old bar?"

"The critter was all of twelve or thirteen years old or I miss my guess."

"The critter? It was an animal? I'm afraid I don't understand."

"The bar cuffed me a few good licks, my leg, my arm, one place and another. The bar. B-e-a-r."

"Oh," she said. Good heavens, the man couldn't even speak the King's English! And she'd thought to transform him?

They turned a corner and saw the labyrinth's exit a few steps ahead. Lightning flashed, thunder rumbled immediately after, and several drops of rain struck Marianne's face.

Harriet looked over her shoulder. "Mr. Clinton told me the most extraordinary story?" she said. "His late father knew Edward, was a great admirer of the earl. That's how Mr. Clinton learned of the Ramsdens and of the Hall, though visiting me wasn't his purpose in journeying to England. While trapping near the Lake of the

Woods in the Canadian wilds, he met a Mr. Astor, an American merchant who harvests animal pelts in North America and markets them all around the world. Mr. Clinton is in London as Mr. Astor's representative, arranging for the sale of his furs."

A purveyor of furs! Marianne thought. *Does he wear that long-tailed fur hat so that he'll be a walking demonstration of his wares?* Mr. Clinton's reason for coming to the Hall seemed harmless, his manner wasn't at all theatening, and in fact, in his inept way, he even seemed to seek her approval. Why, then, had she recoiled so violently when he blocked her path?

Unbidden, a vision appeared in her mind, a picture so clear in every detail she might have mistaken it for a memory of an actual event if she hadn't known better:

Wolf Clinton swept her into his arms and carried her, his helpless prisoner, to a black stallion. He swung into the saddle behind her, spurring the horse, riding recklessly through the moonlit night with one arm tight around her waist, galloping across the fields to a great forest and into the primeval darkness beneath the trees where he dismounted, laying her gently on a bed of fur-scented branches. . . .

The vision faded, and Marianne realized with a start that they had reached the shelter of the Litchfield Hall drawing room. Through the windows, she watched jagged fingers of lightning slash earthward from roiling black clouds. Thunder shook the Hall.

She felt as unsettled as the weather.

"I'll ring for tea?" Harriet said.

"No," Wolf answered unexpectedly. "I must return to the city at once."

"In this storm?" Harriet asked. Rain streaked the windows; a curtain billowed inward. "You must stay until it clears," she told him.

"I should never have come here today," Wolf said. "I was driving past the Hall and decided to call on the spur of the moment. I'm expected at Kravitz's fur warehouse in a few hours."

This time Marianne understood his every word. And, though he glanced at her often, his gaze no longer seemed predatory but strangely uncertain. Why was he unsure of himself? Whatever the reason, she had to admit that Wolfson Clinton's changes of mood intrigued her.

As he was making his farewells, a footman entered the drawing room with a taper and lit the lamps and wall sconces.

"You look so strange," Harriet said when Wolf was gone. "Are you feeling ill?"

"It must be the candlelight." They crossed the room, Marianne sitting in the wing chair next to the fireplace, Harriet on the sofa opposite. "Such an unusual gentleman, Mr. Clinton," Marianne said.

"A fine-looking young man if only he would see fit to enlist the services of a barber and a tailor. I sensed an inner strength to him, a sense of command you find in some military men. Despite his appearance, he's a man other men would

55

follow. Perhaps he soldiered with the Canadians?"

"But at the same time," Marianne said, "did you notice how uneasy he became?"

Harriet smiled knowingly. "He may have expected a savage Indian to spring at him from behind the hedges, not a beautiful young woman."

Marianne reddened. "For some reason, I suspect Mr. Clinton's no stranger to the company of women. There was more than our presence disturbing him, though I have no notion what it could be." *And*, she thought with some regret, *we'll probably never find out.*

"I know!" Harriet clasped her hands in front of her. "Mr. Wolfson Clinton possesses a secret. There's a mystery in his past that he must never reveal, and for some reason, he fears you have the means to uncover it. There must be a skeleton in the wolf's closet."

"An unhappy love affair?" Marianne suggested. "He wasn't really injured by a rampaging bear but in a brawl? If this were one of Lucinda's stories, he would have inadvertantly killed a man in a fight and had to flee his native land. Explaining why he's now in London."

"Whatever it is," Harriet said, "he must be concealing something. Of course, that doesn't make him guilty of wrongdoing; all of us have secrets."

"I don't." As soon as she spoke, Marianne bit her lip. Wasn't she keeping the circumstances of her father's death a secret?

"Then, you're most unusual. Even I have a small secret," Harriet admitted, "in the form of an unexpected visitor to Litchfield Hall. You'll never guess who he was if I don't give you a hint. This gentleman called on me last week to ask me to be a sponsor for a society he's helping to organize. 'The Society for Returning Young Woman from London to Their Friends in the Country' is, I do believe, its name."

"General Stansbury! It could be no one else." Marianne smiled. "And I suspect the general's visit here belies an interest in more than the welfare of young women who have lost their way in the city. He's been like a ship adrift since his wife passed on."

"Well," Harriet said, lowering her eyes, "the exact nature of his interest must, I suppose, be the general's secret, at least for the time being. Although he did invite me to accompany you to *Macbeth* on Thursday next. Of course, I declined his invitation with thanks."

"I wonder," Marianne said, "what the ton would say if the general included our Mr. Clinton in his invitation?"

"They'd conclude the general's war wounds had caused him to lose his senses."

Harriet was right, Marianne told herself, it wouldn't do at all. She must be the one in danger of losing her senses. . . .

The next night, tossing and turning on her bed of down, Marianne recalled her visit to Litchfield Hall, smiling at Harriet's admission of General Stansbury's interest. Gradually her smile changed to a frown. How could she account for her own impulses, her viewing Mr. Clinton as a challenge, a man to be remade, and the way her thoughts returned to him again and again?

Believing nothing to be a better distraction from her own confusion than an account of the trials and tribulations of others, she took *Midnight Weddings* from her bedside table. After reading a few pages she dozed off. . . .

She walked amidst tropical growth where water dripped from dark green leaves and red, orange, and blue birds called raucously from high branches. The fetid air reeked with a nameless odor, a rank moist smell of dampness and decay. A snake undulating along a vine sent a tremor of fear down her spine.

Climbing to the top of a low knoll, she parted a veil of hanging moss and saw sunlight slanting into a glade where it formed a halo around a gilded carriage. As the sounds of the jungle stilled, a rich perfume enticed her forward. Marianne approached the carriage slowly, drawn against her will.

The door swung open, seemingly of its own volition, and a hand in a chicken-skin glove reached toward her, the curved fingers beckoning. As she watched, the fabric of the glove split asunder to reveal a dark and hairy paw.

She awoke gasping for breath, trembling as she stared fearfully into the midnight darkness of her room.

Chapter Five

Lord Brandon, his identity concealed by a flowing black cape and an oversized, broad-brimmed hat, entered the rear of the Covent Garden pit just as the curtain fell at the conclusion of the one-act. The audience rewarded the performance with a smattering of applause, several raucous hoots of disapproval, and widespread indifference.

Ignoring the jostling of the groundlings, Lord Brandon kept his gaze fixed on a box in the second tier directly above the stage's left exit. On the wall to one side of the box, an oil chandelier glowed, highlighting the diagonal gilt stripes of the theater's decor; to the other side was the maroon velvet curtain.

They were all present and accounted for, Lord Brandon noted, General Stansbury and Georgie on the upper row, Lucinda and Marianne in the lower. Merely looking at Marianne made his heart leap. Incomparable! Those bewitching black curls, the deep blue eyes, that saucy hat with the provocative plume, the enchanting pale blue gown with the ruffle around the décolletage.

He wrenched his gaze away. He must keep his eyes on Georgie, not Marianne, so that he wouldn't miss his friend's signal that the time had come for the two of them to meet. He needed to know whether Marianne suspected his deception, and it was up to Georgie to find out. Would Georgie inadvertantly let the cat out of the bag? If he did, the impersonation of Wolf Clinton must end at once.

All four were animated, Lord Brandon saw, even the usually taciturn general. Georgie kept glancing at Lucinda and then looking quickly away. Was Georgie in danger of losing his heart to a female scribbler? Lord Brandon shook his head in wonderment at the strange partialities of his fellow men. But if that was what Georgie wanted, so be it.

Lord Brandon grew impatient; waiting and watching vexed him. If only he were in the box instead of in the pit. What were they saying now? Were they talking about him? He'd give a pretty penny to know. . . .

"Never saw Kemble as Macbeth," George said. "Hear he's a wonder in the part."

"Humph," the general commented. The years had added gray to the general's dark hair, a not unattractive solidity to his frame, and an outspoken certainty to his opinions. Emulating Wellington, he wore an old blue frock coat.

Marianne couldn't help smiling to herself. Whatever Georgie said, the general contradicted. Since his near-fatal injury at Waterloo, the general had devoted himself to his improving societies and to encouraging his only son to follow a military career.

"In Mr. Kemble's lexicon," the general went on, "'bird' becomes 'beard,' 'virgin' is 'vargin' and a 'leap' is transformed into a 'lep.' Worst of all, he twists Shakespeare's 'aches' into an unrecognizable 'aitches.'"

"Have to admire the chap," George said with a glance at his father. "Goes his own way, no matter what. Who knows how the Bard pronounced 'aches'?"

"I know how he didn't pronounce the word; he didn't say 'aitches.'"

Marianne interceded. "Last week I met a gentleman," she said, "who insisted on calling a bear a bar. He quite confused me at first."

George leaned forward abruptly. "Who was this?" he asked.

"A Mr. Wolfson Clinton. You've heard of him?"

George blinked several times, sat back in his chair, took a handkerchief and dabbed at his face. What was the matter with him? Marianne wondered.

"Better than that," George said at last. "Talked with the chap. Came to my lodgings armed with a letter of introduction. Quite an extraordinary

61

fellow." George started to go on, hesitated, then finally asked, "Pray tell, Miss Marianne, what did you think of him?"

"He was hardly the uncouth creature Lord Brandon made him out to be."

George raised his eyebrows. "Not my impression. Reminded me of a bear let loose in a Piccadilly tea room."

"I've heard so much about this Mr. Wolfson Clinton," Lucinda broke in, "that I'm all aflutter to meet him face to face. Would I swoon from fright? Would I be transported by rapture?"

"One thing's for certain," Marianne said. "He could use the services of either Mr. John Philip Kemble or Mr. Edmund Kean."

George looked startled. "You suspect this Clinton of playing a part and playing it poorly?" he blurted.

"A part?" Marianne asked in bewilderment. "No, of course not. That isn't to say he couldn't learn to play the part of a gentleman. Mr. Kemble is able to change his demeanor from role to role, making each in turn believable, surely Mr. Clinton could learn to master the words and actions of a man of society."

"Miss Harriet informs me he's a Canadian," the general said. "I commanded a regiment of Canadians in '98. Or was it '99? No, it was '98. A stouthearted lot, every man jack of them. Had minds of their own, so they needed discipline and training. We could have good use of their kind at Waterloo."

"Training." Marianne seized the word. "Education. If Mr. Clinton had someone to help him, think how it might improve his lot both in the fur trade and in society."

"Don't like it," George said, "don't like it one whit. Man won't be in London that long; soon be on his way to Paris or wherever."

"Why, Georgie," Lucinda said, "you surely seem to know a great deal about him."

George reddened and shook his head. "No more than the next man," he said.

"We're beholden to Mr. Clinton in a way," Marianne said, "since his father befriended the earl of Litchfield while the earl was traveling on foreign soil. You should try to help him make his way in London, Georgie. There's so much you could show him."

"You could give the man pointers in the art of gaming," the general remarked drily, "providing this Mr. Clinton is plump in the pocket."

George shook his head vigorously. "Not the thing at all, Miss Marianne," he said. "Lord Brandon wouldn't like it."

"I, for one," Marianne told him, "don't care a jot for Lord Brandon's opinion on the matter."

"Why, Georgie." Lucinda's voice showed her surprise. "I'm quite astounded you don't want to help the poor man. It's not like you at all."

George shifted uncomfortably as all three turned to look at him, running his finger under his collar as though to give himself more breathing room. "Might introduce him to my tailor," he mumbled. "Name's Taylor, by the bye."

"Certainly you could," Lucinda said. "And

invite him as your guest at the Cocoa Tree and at Jackson's. It would lend a cachet to his presence in London."

"Doubt if he'd be interested," George said. "Doubt it very much." He brightened. "Needs more than a cachet. Needs things best taught by women. The dance, manners, the art of conversation."

"*I* could help him," Marianne said slowly. "It wouldn't be easy, and I'd require his consent since he'd have to want to make something of himself if he's to succeed. What a challenge it would be!" She looked at the others. "What do you all think?" she asked.

General Stansbury pondered his reply. First and foremost, he believed a campaign to civilize this Wolfson Clinton was a preposterous notion, one likely to lead to disappointment and possibly disaster. On the other hand, he hadn't become a skilled military tactician by playing the fool. Over the years, he'd discovered his opposition to a scheme—last Saturday's unfortunate stilt race, for instance—more often than not caused young people to embrace it. He could judge matters of this sort objectively except when they concerned his son.

He couldn't be objective about George for one simple reason. Beneath his bluster, despite his disappointment that the boy hadn't followed in his footsteps, he loved his son.

This plan to remake Mr. Clinton involved George only peripherally. Therefore the general found himself able to come down squarely on the fence.

"Not much taken with the idea," he said to Marianne. "Can't do too much harm, either, I suppose."

"In one of my novels, perhaps," Lucinda said, "a crude colonial could be fashioned into a gentleman, but in real life the difficulties pile one upon the other."

"It's true I'd probably need to ask for Georgie's help." Marianne directed her remark more to Lucinda than to the others.

Lucinda looked at her. "You *are* an excellent tutor," she said slowly. "Any help you gave Mr. Clinton would be better than his having none at all."

"A romp," George said without his customary enthusiasm. "Set the ton on its ear. Picture the scene. A masquerade ball at Carleton House, a horrible squeeze. Mr. Clinton enters, the ladies stare, the gentlemen seethe with envy. Clinton reveals his true identity. He's not a gentleman at all; he's a Canadian. A sensation."

The Covent Garden curtain began to rise, the babble of talk and laughter lessened, and the audience settled back, an expectant hush falling over the theater.

"I could do it," Marianne said thoughtfully. Her speech quickened, "I want to do it; I should do it." The words came in a rush, "Georgie, ask him if he's willing. Tell Mr. Clinton I shall do it, I shall, I shall."

Thunder rumbled from offstage. "When shall we three meet again?" the First Witch asked. "In thunder, lightning, or in rain?"

"When the hurlyburly's done," the Second Witch replied, "when the battle's lost and won."

George waited until the play was well under way before slipping through the door at the rear of their box. He walked down a long corridor and descended stairs to the pit level, where he stood listening to the barely audible words coming from the distant stage.

A hand gripped his arm. "In here." Lord Brandon took him to an alcove in the corridor leading to the entrance.

George blinked when he looked at his friend. "Hat's much too large for you, Brandon," he said. "Covers your ears."

"So no one will ask why my hair has suddenly become as black as pitch."

"Didn't wear the beard tonight. Could have come as Clinton, after all."

"Firstly, Georgie, the curst beard itches like the very devil. Secondly, I don't want you seen talking to Wolf Clinton. In the ton, tittle-tattle travels like lightning. Tell me, does she or doesn't she?"

"Magnificent, Brandon, you must have been magnificent at Litchfield Hall. Marianne suspects nothing. Not the shadow of a doubt. What a hum this is, Brandon."

Lord Brandon nodded. "It's clear sailing, then. Lucinda Beattie won't think to question who Clinton is. Old Mrs. Featheringill may be a higher hurdle; the old lady's as sharp as one of her needles. Knows my father, and there's a family resemblance."

"Miss Lucinda looked charming tonight, don't you agree? The rose of her gown, the bloom in her cheeks. Dash it all, Brandon, you have to help me. Can't think of a word to say when Lucinda and I are alone. Tongue's tied in twenty knots. Always that way around women."

"There's one thing females always like to do," Lord Brandon told him, "and that's give advice. Everyone knows the general wants you to be an officer and all, that the two of you are at odds more often than not. If they didn't before your stilt race, they do now."

"The stilt race! Brandon, I ask you, would you expect to encounter a cart loaded with night soil on St. James Street at midday?"

"Hardly. I'll wager even money Chichester had something to do with that cart being where it was. He's a sly one, Chi is."

"And to have the general leaving White's just as I was trying to climb out of the muck. Not only the general, the duke of Wellington, too!"

"I never did hear what the general said. Did he stop to introduce you to the duke?"

"Hardly likely. Never acknowledged me. Rode off. Holding his nose."

"Rotten luck all around," Lord Brandon commiserated. "As I said, ask Lucinda for advice. Mind now, Georgie, don't *take* her advice, merely discuss it, pro and con, raise objections, speculate on your possible success or failure. Could spin on for weeks, perhaps months. Her being a scribbler, she ought to have suggestions gleaned from her fictions. She's probably an avid reader as well."

"Don't hold it too much against her, Brandon, her being a female novelist and all."

"Georgie, upon my word I don't. I believe each of us, every man and woman, is entitled to one flaw. Consider Shakespeare's heroes; Hamlet can't make up his mind; Othello is madly jealous; Macbeth takes advice from his wife. We have to overlook one failing in people."

George brightened. "Hadn't looked at it that way before. Don't think Lucy has any other flaws." He raised an eyebrow. "Even Marianne? Even she has a flaw?"

"She's no exception to the rule, sad to say. Marianne has faulty judgement. Didn't I offer for her? Didn't she reject me, forcing me into all this?" With his hand, he indicated his broad-brimmed hat and flowing cape. "How much simpler to have said 'yes' and have done with it."

"Marianne. Almost forgot. I tried to stop her, Brandon, but couldn't."

"Stop her from doing what?"

"She proposes to make you over. For your own good."

"Make me over?"

"Not you, actually. Wolfson Clinton. Sees more than one flaw in him. Wants me to instruct him in fashion, gaming, proper speech. Intends to introduce him into society or some such folderol. Should have told her women have coming outs, not men."

"George." Lord Brandon called his friend

"George" only when he became especially vexed with him. Not angry, only vexed, he could never find it in himself to be angry with George. "George," he said again, "you seem to be telling me she proposes to turn Wolf Clinton into a man of fashion. And you couldn't dissaude her?"

"That's the size of it, Brandon. Did all I could."

"Don't you see the peril? The closer Wolf Clinton comes to being fashionable, the more he resembles me. And therefore the greater the odds that my scheme will unravel. And once I'm discovered, all my chances for winning Marianne will be damaged beyond repair."

"Dash it, Brandon, I should have tried harder. Had her mind set on it, you see. Sorry if I've been cork-brained. But there it is."

"That abominable beard's the worst risk. Marianne will do her utmost to force Clinton to shave it off. The unmasking would be fatal. I'll have to come up with a good excuse to spurn the razor."

"A Clinton family malady? A hideous birthmark?"

"I'll think of something." Lord Brandon pointed an admonishing finger at his friend. "Remember this," he told him, "and remember it well. When I'm in the guise of Wolf Clinton, I *am* Wolf Clinton. You're to treat me as you would a stranger from the wilds of Canada, not as you'd treat Lord Brandon and not as you might treat Lord Brandon masquerading as Mr. Clinton. Do you understand me, Georgie?"

"Absolutely. No question." He frowned. "Who are you now?"

69

"I'm Lord Brandon."

"Good. Wanted you to know, Lord Brandon, I plan to make an appointment for Mr. Clinton with William Taylor of Bury Street. Thought you might let him know."

"Taylor's notions of toggery aren't quite mine. Why don't you—?"

"Pass the word along to Clinton, that's a good fellow."

"Sometimes you go too far." Lord Brandon sighed and capitulated. "All right, Georgie, I'll inform friend Clinton." He drew in a deep breath. "You'll be happy to learn the odor from the night soil is almost gone." Lord Brandon slapped George affectionately on the shoulder. "Enjoy *Macbeth*," he said, touching the brim of his hat in a farewell salute.

George watched him until he disappeared around a turn in the corridor. From the stage came the voice of John Philip Kemble declaiming as Macbeth. *Beware*, George wanted to warn the Scottish thane, *trouble's brewing all about you. And you, Brandon, best not take Miss Marianne too lightly, best watch your step. Even without stilts you're likely to end facedown in the muck.*

Chapter Six

Because the afternoon was cool for the middle of May, the top of the landau was up, and so Marianne didn't see Brabson, her coachman, rein in the team of matched bays. She did notice the slowing of the Hilton green and gold carriage and the diminished clatter of the wheels on the cobbles as they came to a halt in front of the tailor shop at 32 Bury Street.

Leaning forward to look through the landau's side window, she caught sight of George Stansbury, resplendent in a green tailcoat, pacing back and forth in front of the shop. "Georgie's here to meet us," she told Lucinda, "but I see no evidence of Mr. Clinton."

Lucinda straightened her yellow and blue bonnet. "I'm so thrilled at the prospect of my first look at him."

Marianne smiled, knowing full well Lucinda's flutter was most certainly not due to Wolf Clinton but to the presence of George Stansbury. She told herself her own eagerness to meet Wolf again was due entirely to the challenge facing her. Was it possible, after all, to change a man?

As soon as Brabson lowered the landau's steps and opened the door, George sketched a bow. "Patience," he advised when asked where Mr. Clinton was. "A final tuck here, a bit of brushing there and he'll be with us. Mr. Taylor's almost finished."

"Mr. Taylor." Marianne repeated the name. "How apt. I only hope Mr. Clinton's given name of Wolfson doesn't proclaim his true nature."

"Never," George protested. "Wants to be a gentleman in the worst way. Jewel in the rough, a regular trump, I'll warrant. Modest man. Can't help liking the chap."

Marianne smiled fondly. "Georgie, you like everyone."

"'Pon my word, I don't. Nasty chap tried to hold my head under water when I was ten. Wager of some sort. During a swimming race. Didn't like him one whit."

"I hope," Marianne said, "that Mr. Clinton's modesty doesn't mean he still hides his face behind his atrocious black beard."

"Higgins did what he could. Higgins, my valet, you know. Any minute now. Have to hurry them along. With your pardon." Bowing, George left them and returned to the inside of the shop.

He reemerged in a matter of moments, leaving the door ajar behind him. Smiling, he strode to the landau, glancing over his shoulder before handing Marianne and Lucinda to the sidewalk, where they stood expectantly watching the shop entrance.

George held up both arms as though quieting a cheering multitude. "May I present," he announced, "the new and natty Mr. Wolfson Clinton."

Wolf walked uncertainly from the dimness of the tailor shop into the sunlight. Stopping a few feet from them, he blinked before looking at Marianne as though seeking her approval and hers only, then gazed past her in the general direction of a linen draper's on the other side of Bury Street.

Marianne, at first pleasantly surprised at the change in Wolf's appearance, quickly decided she'd judged too soon. Wolf Clinton had been transformed; he was no longer the savage from the Canadian wilds. He was slender and stylish, very much the young English gentleman of fancy. Except. . . .

The three of them surrounded Wolf, inspecting him and his new garb.

"Knitted wool pantaloons," George informed Marianne. "All the rage of this season. Trouser straps under the insteps of the shoes. Quite up to snuff."

"The blue of his tailcoat matches the blue of his eyes," Lucinda observed.

Marianne shook her head. "The beard, he still wears the beard. It's been trimmed, I'll grant you that, and the cut could be considered distinguished; but it's not in the London style. He could pass, perhaps, for a statesman from Vienna or a count from Budapest; he's not an English gentleman."

73

Studying the details of Wolf's transfiguration, she began to circle him slowly, followed by Lucinda and George, the three of them scrutinizing Wolf first from one angle and then another.

"Tried to reason with him," George said. "About the beard. Wouldn't listen. Might have been talking to a gate post."

Wolf spoke for the first time. "Like I said, because of bar."

"Means the bear," George explained. "In the western mountains of Canada. Attacked by a grizzled bear, leg cut to ribbons, face slashed. 'Honorable scar,' I said to him. He was having none of it."

If the beard covered a scar, Marianne conceded to herself, perhaps it would have to remain. Still, scars could be attractive, hinting of gallantry, of sabers and cavalry charges. A man certainly didn't come by them playing hazard at the Cocoa Tree.

"I do like the yellow of his pantaloons," Marianne admitted, "instead of the usual tan."

"The yellow of the inexpressibles, you mean," Lucinda corrected her.

From the corner of her eye, Marianne saw George raise his eyebrows at the nicety. Evidently he had no more patience with euphemisms than she did.

"Pantaloons," Marianne insisted. "They are what they are. Prettified language will never change that."

With a tingle of excitement, Marianne noted that Wolf's shoulders were broad, his hips slim, his waistline small, and all without the aid of stays. Most satisfactory for a man of fashion, she thought, assuring herself that that accounted for her otherwise inexplicable frisson.

"The yellow stripes in the neckcloth are exactly the right shade," Lucinda said. "They remind me of primroses. 'A primrose by a river's brim, a yellow primrose was to him, and it was nothing more.'"

"Wordsworth," George said unexpectedly. When the two women turned to look at him, he became flustered. "Favorite of mine," he explained. "Wordsworth."

Wolf remained motionless and without expression as they continued to circle him.

"Ecru gloves," George said, nodding at Wolf's hands. "Blue top hat, curled brim, elegant walking cane."

"He's wearing a watch chain and fob," Marianne said, "but he doesn't appear to have a quizzing glass."

George nodded. "Personal preference, that. His. Mine as well. All in all, he'll make a hit, a palpable hit."

"He is quite dashing," Lucinda agreed.

"I have to admit," Marianne said, "except for the beard, I'm more than satisfied. My congratulations to Mr. Taylor. And to you, Georgie." *Yes*, she told herself, *I can finish what Georgie has so well begun.* Smiling a little, she pictured how confounded Lord Brandon would be when he learned of her accomplishment.

Wolf Clinton raised his black walking cane, held it in front of him at arm's length and swung slowly around in a circle, the sweep of the cane forcing the two women and George to step back.

"Tattersall's," Wolf's deep voice rumbled.

"Tattersall's?" Marianne echoed, surprised he knew the name.

"Yearling auction," George said hastily. "I took Wolf there yesterday. I can testify he's a nonpareil when it comes to judging horseflesh."

Wolf turned to face Marianne, thrusting his cane at her so the tip came to within an inch of her nose. "I ain't," he said, "a horse to be led about, turned this way and that, examined and commented on. Do you take me for a black gelding? Do you have a mind to step closer to examine my teeth before making your bid?" He bared his teeth.

Marianne stared in astonishment, blinking at the glint of the sun on the metal tip of the walking cane, looking past the cane at Wolf Clinton. She was taken aback by the anger darkening his blue eyes.

She drew in a tremulous breath. "A gentleman," she said with frost coating her voice, "does not point his walking cane at a lady."

"Don't you remember, milady?" Wolf asked. "I'm no gentleman. I'm here because I ain't."

The heat of Marianne's anger melted her armor of cool disdain. "Don't be insolent," she snapped. Glancing at Lucinda, she said, "I think it's time for us to return home," and started to walk to the landau.

Wolf stepped back, managing at the same time to block her path. Marianne stopped, looking up at him, her fury rooting her to the spot.

Ever so deliberately Wolf walked around her, boldly studying her. George and Lucinda seemed to recede from her vision, to become a blur, until she was conscious only of Wolf Clinton. She and Wolf were tethered one to the other by the intensity of their mutual anger, joined as though by galvanic electrical impulses crackling between them that others could intrude on only at their peril.

Wolf flicked his cane at her gown like a schoolmaster using his rod to draw attention to an unusual exhibit. He meant to mock her, did he? Very well, she'd give as good as she got. Or better.

Mimicking her voice, he said, "White dresses are all the fashion in London this year, I observe."

Marianne banked the flames of her anger. In her dealings with men, ice usually proved a more effective weapon than fire. She'd answer with a precise description of her attire and let him make what he would of it.

"My gown is of white striped silk," she informed him coolly, "with a double row of green ruffles slightly above a proper, ankle-length hem."

"Damme, you're fond of green," he went on, "green shoes, green jacket, green umbrella," pointing with his cane, and pointing, and pointing once more.

No matter how he goaded her, she was determined not to allow him to provoke her into losing her temper. She was perfectly able to control her feelings.

"I'm wearing green kid slippers," she said, "a

green linen spencer, and carrying a long-handled parasol of white silk trimmed with green and gold."

Wolf nodded, accepting her description.

"You should understand," she told him in a voice edged with sarcasm, "it is *de rigueur* in polite society to compliment a lady on her appearance."

Wolf's searching gaze roved appraisingly from the toes of her slippers to the uppermost curve of the brim of her fashionable bonnet. He gave an exaggerated sigh. "Mesmerizing," he intoned.

He had no need for a quizzing glass, she decided; his voice mocked her all too well without help. She said nothing, determined to appear detached and ladylike despite her outrage. His remarks on her appearance would now undoubtedly decline into inanities she could answer with scorn or else ignore, as she chose. If not, their skirmishing would spread until it exploded in a conflagration so intense it would release her, allowing her to turn her back on him for good.

"And what is your hat called?" he asked.

"It's often referred to as a poke bonnet. The trim is green ivy."

"A poke bonnet," he repeated. "We use pokes of a different sort in Canada, put them 'round the necks of horses to stop the critters from jumping over fences. Your poke is something akin to the blinders on a horse. I can think of only one thing such a bonnet might prevent a man from doing."

How insolent he was! There was no reason she should hesitate to answer in kind. "I daresay you refer to kissing. You think, perhaps, they're to shield women from temptation. If that were indeed their reason for being and all men possessed your charm, no woman would have to wear a poke bonnet.''

Wolf smiled wickedly. ''What I meant,'' he said, ''was that the bonnet makes it more difficult to view your face and hair. Leaving me and all men the losers.''

She had misjudged him; he had been hoaxing her all along, and she had let him lead her on. In the future, though she doubted there would be a future for them, she'd be more wary. Now all she managed to say, and weakly at that, was ''I daresay you believe being transformed into a man of the first stare of fashion entitles you to air your opinions.''

''Got your back up, did I? I meant to be gallant like Mr. Stansbury told me to be. 'Twasn't me who thought of the kissing.''

''Any more of your gallantry and I'll be ready for a fit of the dismals.''

His gaze left her bonnet, his eyes lingering on her face before proceeding lower to the creamy semi-circle revealed above the scooped ruff of her gown's neckline. Again he paused in his scrutiny before his gaze roamed lower still.

''The waists of English women must be positioned uncommonly high,'' he said. ''In Canada they're placed more where men's are.''

''Ever since my mother's day,'' Marianne told him, doing her best to ignore the strange tingling his gaze provoked, ''and that was more than twenty years ago, waists have been rising for all of us unwilling to be dowdies. To my eyes, the result is most pleasing."

"If they rise much more, soon they'll make the acquaintance of the neckline of your gown." Wolf smiled. "Of course, certain delightful obstacles will prevent that."

"Sir, you forget yourself!" Marianne's face flushed crimson; her voice trembled with unbridled anger.

"You object to my nicety of language?" Again he mimicked her.

"You were right; you're not a gentleman. What's more, you never will be one, not in a hundred years. Now pray let me pass."

Wolf, not budging, met her withering gaze unflinchingly. She couldn't tell from his expression if he was surprised into immobility by the violence of her attack or whether he was too stubborn to yield.

"Let me pass." Her voice rose as she brandished her parasol like a sword.

For an instant she thought he intended to treat her gesture as a challenge and duel her, his walking cane against her parasol. All at once his humor seemed to change, and lowering the cane, he removed his top hat in a clumsy left-handed salute and stepped away.

She swept past him without a glance. "Lucinda," she said over her shoulder, "we are leaving. Brabson, drive us home. At once."

Ignoring a bewildered George, who tried in vain to offer her his hand, she climbed into the landau and sat stiffly in the far corner. After helping Lucinda, George hesitated with his hand on the open door.

"Dash it all, don't be hasty," he pleaded with Marianne. "Man's not a scapegrace. Means to keep the line, you know. Doesn't know how. The devil's soft in his tongue. Not his fault."

"Close the door, Georgie," Marianne told him. "I'm certain you'll find a means to transport Mr. Clinton back to his lair. There must be a cage for hire somewhere. You might ask one of the chair men."

"Only proves he needs our help."

"Not mine." Marianne tapped on the roof with the tip of her parasol, and the carriage jolted forward.

"Hold!"

The assurance in Wolf Clinton's voice made Brabson pull back on the ribbons, bringing the landau to a sudden halt.

"My lady," the reinsman called down to Marianne, "pray forgive me. Shall I go on?"

By this time Wolf had the steps down and the door to the carriage open. Marianne retreated farther into her corner, expecting him to leap into the landau, but Wolf held, his gaze intent on her, his look challenging her. Again she experienced that unusual frisson—of annoyance, she was certain. Yet, try as she might, she couldn't deny something about the man appealed to her.

She wouldn't oppose him, she decided, not directly. That wasn't the way to deal with Mr. Clinton or any other man. Women carried the day by using their patience, imagination and intelligence. Men might declaim and posture, rage and bluster; women persevered and, in the end, triumphed. That was the way of the world.

Without immediately answering Brabson, she turned to Lucinda and said, "I'm quite overset, so I don't wish any additional contretemps." She glanced above her in the direction of the box where Brabson sat. "What will the ton think of us?" she whispered.

"To avoid further upset," Lucinda suggested, "you could invite the two gentlemen to accompany us as far as Mr. Stansbury's lodgings."

"Georgie." Marianne ignored Wolf. "If you and your acquaintance would care to join us."

"Pleasure!" George climbed aboard and sat across from them, Wolf taking a place at his side. Once more they started on their homeward journey.

Marianne waited for a crow of triumph from Wolf to celebrate his victory, Pyrrhic though it would prove to be. He remained silent, however. *Good,* she told herself, *he owns he's gone well past the line.* For all she cared he could remain in a shamed miff for the remainder of the trip.

The landau slowed to a stop. When they heard loud shouts of men on the road ahead, Wolf swung open the door and leaned out. "A barrel's fallen from a dray," he reported. "The road's blocked."

A scream of pain sent a sympathetic shiver along Marianne's spine. The cry, though, came not from the street ahead of them but from a nearby town house.

The cry came again.

"That's a child!" Marianne exclaimed.

"Spare the rod," George said, "and spoil the child. Always been the general's maxim."

"This child's in danger." Marianne's tone was urgent. "We must help him."

Wolf vaulted down to the cobbles. "See to the ladies," he told George before striding across the brick walk and climbing the steps to the door of the fashionable building. Somehow, Marianne thought, he looked different. Of course—he hadn't limped.

Still another heart-wrenching cry jolted Marianne. She scrambled past Lucinda and George, clambering down awkwardly to the pavement.

"Wolf," she heard George shout from behind her, "the road's clear."

When she climbed to the small porch, Wolf was pounding on the door with his fist. There was no answer. He opened the door, and looking past him, she saw a chandelier and a curving staircase and caught a glimpse of furniture covered with dust sheets. Wolf stepped inside, but when she started to follow him, he turned to her, scowling and shaking his head.

"Stay outside," he ordered. His voice, she noted, had lost its huskiness.

He shut the door, stranding her on the porch. She hesitated at the top of the steps, wondering what was happening inside the silent house, confident Wolf Clinton would set it to rights. His sense of command, his decisiveness, appealed to her. What a pity he was so uncouth, so raw, so unlearned in the ways of gentlemen. If only he had at least a trace of Lord Brandon's manner. Why, she wondered, did she always want what she couldn't have? Why was she never satisfied with half a loaf? She'd rather risk losing the half in seeking the whole.

"Marianne!" George's shout brought her from her reverie; he stood beside the carriage looking up at her. Reluctantly, she went down the steps and joined him on the sidewalk.

"Taking a deuce of a time." George gazed up at the tall chimney-crowned house. At least they had heard no more cries of pain since Wolf disappeared inside.

At long last he appeared, not in the front door but at the head of an alleyway running beside the house.

"His new clothes," Marianne gasped. "They're ruined!"

Black streaks marred Wolf's pantaloons and tailcoat, and when he held up his hand to gesture them to be patient, she saw dark blotches on his gloves as well.

Wolf turned from them, seeming to talk encouragingly to someone in the alley. With a shrug of exasperation, he walked from their sight but returned almost immediately—with a small begrimed boy. Placing his gloved hand on the boy's back, he urged him across the brick walk to the landau. The boy limped noticeably.

"This is Paul," Wolf announced.

Paul's head was lowered, as though staring down at his dirty bare feet. Marianne was sure she had never seen a filthier human being in her entire life. He had huge brown eyes set in a thin soot-blackened face, dirty black hair, narrow shoulders, and spindly legs. Though he wore a nondescript shirt and wrinkled trousers, her impression was that the grime visible on his face, hands, and feet covered his entire body. He smelled vaguely of smoke.

"His master says the boy lives in Spitalfields," Wolf told them.

"Wretched warren," George said. "One of the hives of the mobility. A climbing boy, I'll wager. Clambers up into the flues to sweep away the soot. Been putting out a chimney fire today by the looks of him."

"At home in Canada," Wolf said, "we do it different. We tie a rope around a goose, stand on the roof of the house and pull the bird up the chimney. The flapping of her wings cleans the flue."

"How cruel," Lucinda said. "The poor goose."

"That's not the whole of it, neither. After the cleaning's done, we cook and eat the goose. England's more humane; I suspect here you rarely eat the climbing boy for supper."

Marianne gave Wolf a reproachful stare. "He's so terribly young," she said. "He can't be more than five."

"His master, a Mr. Jeremiah Moles, thinks he's six." Wolf lifted the dirty boy into his arms. "He limps from having pins stuck in the soles of his feet. Encourages the boy to climb quicker, according to Mr. Moles."

"Foul," George said. "Despicable."

"We can't stand by," Marianne said, "and let him mistreat the boy."

"Have no fear," Wolf said, "Mr. Moles ain't going to hurt the lad again."

"Gave the man a good thrashing, I expect," George said.

Wolf shook his head.

"Why won't he hurt the boy again?" Marianne asked.

"'Cause I bought the boy."

They stared at Wolf in disbelief. "You bought him?" Marianne repeated.

"Paid ten pounds. You look flabbergasted. Did Mr. Moles cheat me? Should I have offered him five and settled for seven or eight? Is that the way of you English?"

"In this day and age," Marianne protested, "you can't just buy someone. In America or in Canada, perhaps, but this, after all, is England."

"The lad's a foundling," Wolf told her. "Left as a babe with a church warden in Spitalfields. Brought to the church by a servant in livery, Mr. Moles' story has it, along with a generous gift of money. The warden apprenticed Paul to Mr. Moles as soon as he was able to earn his keep. When the lad was four or so."

During all this time Paul had kept his eyes downcast. Marianne knelt beside him. "The poor boy," she said. "See the sores on his elbows and knees. From climbing up the narrow flues, I expect."

"Mr. Moles seemed happy to sell him once he

heard the price," Wolf said, "for he don't hold out high hopes for the lad's future as a chimneysweep. Too lazy, Mr. Moles claimed. And soon he'll grow too big for the work, providing he survives another year or two. Course I don't own him outright; he's my apprentice. In the fur trade."

Wolf paused as if debating whether to say more. After a moment he did, though tentatively. "Maybe I bought him on account of the way I was brought up myself—" He stopped. "In the wilderness. Not that it wasn't a better place to grow up than here."

Marianne stood, impulsively reached for Wolf's hand and clasped it. "You did the right thing," she told him. "We'll take the boy home and give him a good bath." She held out her gloved hand, now darkened by soot, to the boy. "Come with me, Paul," she said.

Paul shrank away.

"Boy!" Wolf raised his voice, though his tone was not unkind. "Get into the carriage with Miss Hilton."

Paul scrambled up the steps, and Lucinda guided him to a seat beside her.

"The thought of a bath probably frightens him," Marianne said.

"In Canada where I come from," Wolf told the boy, "we always take a bath once a week, on Saturday night, whether we need it or not."

Paul stared at him in total disbelief.

"From now on you'll do the same," Wolf added as he joined them in the landau.

"Dash it all, Wolf," George said as they started off, "I daresay London has hundreds of boys like him. Can't help them all, you know."

Wolf nodded. "I don't mean to, mate," he said. "I just reckon to help one. This one. My friend, Paul, here."

Marianne felt a rush of tenderness for Wolf, sensing the Canadian meant what he said, truly meant every word. Despite his rough exterior, his heart was good and true. He deserved her help. Though he might frighten her, be insolent to her, anger her, unloose unwelcome and disturbing emotions in her, she couldn't turn her back on him. Just as he had been unable to turn his on Paul.

Wolf—Lord Brandon—didn't meet Marianne's tender gaze, looking instead from the window at a pair of dandies—Chichester and Boynton, by God—talking and laughing as they strolled toward the Cocoa Tree. He experienced a pang of regret.

He had meant what he said about helping Paul—that fellow Moles was an abomination—but in truth he had done it for Marianne. If they married, what else might she expect him to do? Marriage to her wouldn't be quite what he, in his amiable selfishness, had envisioned; he'd be forced to give up a great deal. While arrangements could be made for Paul, would be made for him, already he inwardly acknowledged a responsibility toward the lad. He'd be a hundred times more responsible for children of his own; they might even become a burden.

Strange, he'd never considered those aspects of marriage before. Until this very moment, court-ship had been a sport for him, a game to be won or lost. Now he realized it was more, much more. He stood at a divide in the roadway of his life, a fork where the signposts were blurred and indistinct.

Lord Brandon sighed and looked behind the landau, but Chichester and Boynton were no longer in view. They had turned one way, he another. For the first time in his life, in this city he knew and loved so well, he felt alone and lost.

Chapter Seven

The three women sat in the Hilton library in the early afternoon, Marianne intent on her needlework, Lucinda writing at the desk in the center of the room, and old Mrs. Featheringill nodding at the ingleside. Every so often Mrs. Featheringill would waken, her head rising in a series of starts, and stare around the room as if uncertain where she was.

More and more of late, Marianne had noticed with distress, her eighty-year-old great-aunt confused past with present, her reveries with actualities. Fortunately, Marianne consoled herself, the old woman remained content and cheerful in the late autumn of her life.

The book room where Mrs. Featheringill often dozed away the afternoons could only help compound her confusion. Many years ago it had been the favored retreat of Marianne's father and his father before him, a dark and masculine room still smelling vaguely of pipe tobacco and dogs, a room of oak paneling and bookshelves crammed full of ordered rows of leather-bound volumes, of brick hearth and fireplace, of pipe racks and humidors on the tables, hunting scenes on the walls and a stag's antlered head above the mantel.

In recent years Oriental vases and French porcelain figurines had invaded the room in company with Gothic and romantic novels by female authors and a hotchpotch of improving books. From the east wall the portrait of a bygone Hilton patriarch gazed in disapproval at an *arriviste* painting of four plump, diaphanously clad nymphs dancing hand-in-hand around the statue of a pagan god.

Lucinda dipped her quill in the inkwell on the desk, copied a few lines from the open book in front of her and then looked up. "I find many of Mr. Wordsworth's sentiments disturbing," she said, "yet his descriptions of Nature can be quite beautiful."

Marianne, engrossed in her needlework, replied with an encouraging, "Ummm."

"'The rainbow comes and goes,'" Lucinda quoted, "'and lovely is the rose.'"

"Are you still fashioning your poems after Mr. Wordsworth?" Since completing her Ramsden novel and delivering it by hand to Trotter and Sons, Lucinda had been writing poetry to assuage her feeling of emptiness.

"I have been ever since a line in Mrs. More's latest book suggested the method to me. I copy a few verses from Mr. Wordsworth and then substitute my words for his until I become familiar with his meter. These are my lines: 'Georgie comes and goes, and handsome are his clothes.'"

Marianne concealed a smile. Never would she hurt Lucinda's feelings, but though she could admire her prose, poetry was another matter altogether. "Georgie will certainly enjoy a poem praising him in the meter of his favorite poet," she said.

"I wouldn't dare show it to him. My lines have none of the ring of Mr. Wordsworth's, but with practice I hope to improve."

"Is Georgie of the handsome clothes planning to attend our musical evening next week?" Marianne asked.

"Oh, yes, and the general will be here as well. They're both agog to hear your Mr. Wolfson Clinton demonstrate his mastery of the language of the ton before an unsuspecting audience."

"He's not *my* Mr. Clinton."

"No more, I fear, than George Stansbury is my George Stansbury," Lucinda said ruefully. "Did you know the general favors Harriet Ramsden?"

"I suspected as much. She seems flattered by his attentions yet unsure how she should respond."

"He's quite smitten. Georgie sought my counsel yesterday when he and Mr. Clinton were here, my advice concerning his dealings with his father and also the general's suit. Is that an advance for me, do you think? Gentlemen usually ask my help in furthering their own amatory affairs while Georgie seeks my help for his father's."

"I take it as an encouraging sign," Marianne assured her. "If your advice is good, it won't harm your cause; if poor, it won't be resented."

"There's so much I'd like to tell Georgie if only I could write the words instead of speaking them. When I'm with him, I can't think of what to say."

"You must praise him. Men never tire of hearing their praises sung; no compliment is so extreme they consider it ludicrous or repeated so often they find it boring. With men of the ton, nothing succeeds like excess."

"Women enjoy compliments equally well." Lucinda smiled. "The general, however, is much more forthright. No poetry, no high-flown compliments, he doesn't believe in flights of fancy; he intends to storm Litchfield Hall and lay siege to Harriet Ramsden's heart."

"I'm afraid Mr. Wolfson Clinton would applaud the general's plan of campaign."

"I told Georgie," Lucinda said, "to try to make his father understand that waging war and making love are not the same. In war, if the besieged takes flight, you carry the day, while in love, if she flees, you lose all."

Marianne laid her needlework aside. "Mr. Clinton has all the subtlety of a battering ram attacking the gates of a castle. I never thought I'd admit it, but in a way I miss Lord Brandon. He's still not returned from Bath?"

"No, not as yet, though Georgie informs me Lord Brandon will be back in London in time to attend the Prince's Midsummer Ball."

"Ah, it would be a true test for Mr. Clinton, bringing him face to face with Lord Brandon. Since Brandon saw him in his uncivilized state when he disembarked, he may well be able to recognize him when he sees him again. Lord Brandon isn't a man who's easily hoaxed."

Marianne recalled the last time she'd seen Lord Brandon, the day she'd refused his offer of marriage. She missed him even more than she was willing to admit to Lucinda. In spite of his faults, she enjoyed his company, since, in addition to his charm, she found him to be a reasonable man and a reasoning man.

Weren't his faults also the faults of most of the men she knew? Idleness, inconstancy, gaming, eating and drinking were their usual pursuits. What else was there for a gentleman of the ton to spend his life doing? Wasn't Lord Brandon, in fact, very much like her own father?

Her father, so charming, so well loved. Marianne closed her eyes, and a chill shivered along her spine as she remembered the day so long ago that had changed her life forever. Her father was taking them, her mother and Marianne, to America. Everything would be better in a new world. . . .

From her bedroom window, Marianne saw her grandfather, dressed in top hat and black frock coat, arrive and hurry up the steps. She ran to the stairs and down to the foyer in time to see him go into the drawing room. Dust sheets shrouded the furniture, the fountain was silent, and the trunks sat in the entrance hallway waiting to be carted to the ship.

Marianne ran around the foyer to the partly

open doorway when her mother, inside, screamed. Marianne froze. She heard her mother sobbing. Then her grandfather Hilton's voice, the words indistinct. She edged closer to the doorway, the better to hear him.

"He didn't suffer," her grandfather said. "He died instantly."

Her mother moaned. Panic gripped Marianne. Who? Who had died? Her father? No, it couldn't be her father.

"Terrence fired into the air," her grandfather said. "This man Smith claims he didn't aim to kill. Yet there it is."

It *was* her father. He was dead. She'd never see him again.

"Terry fought the duel to avenge my honor," her mother said.

"Now, Elizabeth, you have to face facts; you know that wasn't the way of it at all. I hate to admit the truth, but Smith was the aggrieved party. Terrence and the man's wife were most indiscreet."

"No." Her mother's voice rose. "He was killed defending my honor." She broke into sobs. "He was, he was."

Marianne turned and stumbled up the stairs to the second floor, opened the door at the end of the hall and climbed to the attic, where she sat on the floor with her back to one of the chimneys. Dead. Her father was dead. He'd betrayed them both. Tears scalded her eyes; she wept.

Lord Brandon is nothing like my father, Marianne told herself, bringing herself back to the present. And yet. . . .

96

Why must her thoughts return time and again to Lord Brandon? He was in Bath; she might never see him again. It would be helpful, though, if he were here to advise her about Mr. Wolfson Clinton. She neither liked nor admired Wolf, personifying as he did so many of the traits she deplored. She listed them to herself: He was arrogant, overbearing, thoughtless, and uncouth, a man who went out of his way to thrust a spoke in her wheel at every turn.

Why, then, did she look forward so eagerly to seeing him again? She must be a gudgeon of the first rank. Perhaps the oddity of the man, his untamed nature, and his unpredictability accounted for her perverse attraction to him. Not to mention his kindness to Paul. Knowing Wolf Clinton, she decided, was akin to reading a novel you didn't particularly enjoy but one you couldn't lay aside until you discovered the ending.

"Not only do I dislike him," Marianne said, "I suspect he may be playing an undergame."

Lucinda paused with her quill in midair. "Lord Brandon?" she asked in surprise.

"No, no, Lord Brandon is an honorable man. I refer to Mr. Wolf Clinton." Marianne frowned. "Don't you find it passing strange the way he arrived in England claiming his father knew the earl of Litchfield? Supposedly he's lived his whole life in Canada, and yet he's hardly mentioned his homeland. And the maze. How easily he found me after I'd lost my way. It was almost as though he'd been there before."

"Harriet may have given him directions for finding his way into the maze."

"Even so, I can't help wondering if he means to

deceive someone. Not just anyone, Harriet and you and I and Georgie, all of us. It's almost as though we were performing in a play. Was it *The Comedy of Errors* where everyone pretended to be someone he wasn't?"

"Perhaps at our musical evening Mr. Clinton will reveal more of his true nature."

"I plan to resolve my suspicions before then, in fact this very afternoon when Georgie brings him here to learn more of the ways of the ton."

"Does Mr. Clinton make a good student?" Lucinda asked.

"When he so chooses. Though he claims to have an ardent desire to improve in order to advance his fur trading interest, he often treats his lessons as larks."

"Ah, larks." Lucinda shook her head. "Young Paul only seems happy when he's whistling in imitation of birds. I can't imagine where he heard them, perhaps while cleaning the flues on the estates of the country gentry."

"Poor Paul. He's so thin, and he seems so downcast no matter what I do." Marianne sighed. "I'd be overjoyed to see him smile but once or twice."

"He walks about the house in a daze, his head down, looking neither right nor left. Almost as if he'd suffered an injury and never completely recovered. You'd think he'd want to make the most of this great chance, be thankful to you and Mr. Clinton for rescuing him from this Mr. Moles. I was a wee bit surprised when you offered to allow him to stay with us for the time being."

"Mr. Clinton's lodgings would never have done. He wouldn't or couldn't prevent the boy from running wild most of the time. I want Paul to have every chance to make something of himself."

"Is it all right if I tell him he can watch our musical evening from the head of the stairs?"

"He'll be bored to tears," Marianne predicted. "Young boys have no taste for such entertainments. But of course he may listen. I only wish I could find something that did interest him."

"If he's not bored, Rolissa Highsmith's singing will surely drive him to bed."

"I was obliged to invite Rolissa, since I particularly want Lord and Lady Kier-Windom to meet Mr. Clinton. If he can impress such a high-in-the-instep pair, our efforts to remake him are succeeding. I'm certain he'll impress Rolissa favorably, since any man under the age of sixty is capable of sending her into paroxysms of giggling delight."

"I suspect Rolissa's a dashing chipper who dampens her muslins at every opportunity." Lucinda looked at Marianne with a worried frown. "Do you imagine she favors Georgie?"

"Of course she does. Now, don't look so stricken, Lucinda. Our dear Rolissa favors all men, particulary those of rank and wealth. But it's no wonder she's such a flirt, the way her mother pushes her forward in the hopes of making a good match. It amazes me Rolissa is able to think of anything other than gentlemen and their prospects."

"I once overheard Chichester describe her as a

Greek goddess descended to Earth," Lucinda said. "As for myself, I'd call her plump. To judge by her mother's figure, Rolissa's greatest circumference will have fallen six inches or more lower by the time she's thirty."

Marianne had never before heard Lucinda be so cutting, and yet she understood her feelings. Men, on the other hand, she would never understand. Here was Lucinda, virtually ignored, while men fought to pay their attentions to Rolissa Highsmith. Were men creatures governed entirely by their baser passions; were they unable to value a woman's grace and intelligence, her loyalty, her goodness, her amiability? If their discrimination was so flawed in selecting a bride, was it any wonder their interest waned after marriage and so many of them formed Other Connections?

Her musings were interrupted by Slater's appearance in the library doorway. "My lady," he said, "this just arrived for you by post."

Marianne removed the billet from Slater's silver salver and slit the sealing wafer. "It's from Lord Brandon in Bath," she told Lucinda, surprised to find her pulses leaping in anticipation.

She eagerly read the message written in Brandon's elegant flowing script:

My Much Esteemed Friend,
Of late I have had the opportunity to give much earnest thought to our unfortunate manner of parting last month. My exceedingly high opinion of you remains constant, if anything it has increased, and nothing

which has happened or will happen in the future will change this fact. Your pleasing demeanor, your beauty, intelligence, taste, and prudence, your kindness and many other excellencies inspire my highest admiration.

If only you would someday permit me to love what I so much admire.

I can bestow my affections only on one who reciprocates them; I will bestow them upon you if you will bestow yours on me; not otherwise, for only mutual love can render either of us happy.

Perhaps I might wish some things were different in you, that you were less impulsive and more reflective, showed no unreasoning prejudice against the male members of the ton, of which I cannot help being a part, and were a shade less stubbornly perverse. Yet these minor matters sink into insignificance in comparison with your many attributes, and especially the whole-souled affection so obviously inherent in you.

While I did not list naivete among your failings, word reaching me here makes me wonder whether I have been remiss in not doing so. It is my understanding, on good authority, that a certain Mr. Wolfson Clinton has recently inserted himself into your circle of acquaintanceship.

Beware of Mr. Clinton!

While I refrain from specifying my objections, since I lack definite proof, my investigations of this "gentleman" are continuing and, when they reach their fruition, be assured I will hasten to advise you of the results.

In the meantime, do not trust him or rely on any of his protestations, since he is not, as I am,

Your obedient servant,
Brandon

How dare he, Marianne asked herself, on the basis of tittle-tattle, tell her what she should do.

Suddenly she remembered that only minutes before, she had wished for Lord Brandon's advice, had, in fact, expressed similar misgivings about Wolf Clinton. Was she, as Lord Brandon claimed, perverse?

She looked up and met Lucinda's questioning gaze. "Lord Brandon condemns me for being impulsive, stubborn, and naive," she told her companion. "Oh, yes, he also warns me of Mr. Clinton's intentions."

"Did I hear my name?"

Startled, Marianne rose to her feet. Wolf Clinton strode into the library, trailing a chagrined Slater in his wake.

"I did my best, my lady," the butler said. "Mr. Clinton would not be gainsaid." He looked darkly at the Canadian.

"I'm certain you did all you could." Marianne noodded her dismissal. "A very dear friend of mine," she told Wolf, "mentioned you in a letter just arrived from Bath."

Wolf glanced at the missive in Marianne's hand.

102

"He pens a stylish script," he said, watching her as she walked to the desk and shut the letter away in a drawer.

"Now, Miss Hilton," Wolf said, "pray tell me if I have this expression right. 'Speak of the devil and he appears.' That is correct, is it not?"

"Entirely correct. Both in the wording and in the appropriateness."

Wolf raised an eyebrow. "One moment." He turned to Lucinda. "I talked to young Paul a few minutes ago. I think he needs help with the Multiplication Table."

"Oh, yes, yes, of course." Lucinda glanced at old Mrs. Featheringill, who, sitting beside the hearth, was leaning forward to peer at Wolf Clinton, her eyes blinking as she seemed to try to place him. "Mr. Stansbury isn't with you?" she asked.

"George," Wolf told her, "was unfortunately detained at the Cocoa Tree about a money matter. He sends his regrets and promises to be present at your musical evening next week." Wolf spoke the words slowly and precisely. Correctly.

Lucinda sighed in disappointment and, with a last look to make sure old Mrs. Featheringill was awake and so a proper chaperone, left the library in search of Paul. Marianne crossed the room to the hearth, where she spoke directly into her great-aunt's ear.

"Mrs. Featheringill," she said loudly, "this is Mr. Wolfson Clinton."

Old Mrs. Featheringill shook her head as though in denial.

Wolf walked to stand in front of her chair, and

103

when she cupped her hand behind her ear, he knelt and, speaking slowly and distinctly, said, "Wolfson Clinton. My name is Wolfson Clinton."

Mrs. Featheringill started to speak, evidently thought better of it, nodded several times and settled back in her chair. Wolf took the old woman's gnarled hand in his, holding it tightly for a few moments while he smiled up at her. Was there an understanding between them? Marianne wondered. No, surely she was mistaken.

Wolf released Mrs. Featheringill's hand, then stood suddenly to face Marianne. His nearness roused feelings she preferred not to have. An odd tingling for one, the beginning warmth of a blush, an awareness of closeness to undefined danger. She stepped back to try to regain her composure.

"The devil was in the bones," Wolf told her.

The devil. With his black beard, Wolf reminded her of a devil, an intriguing, handsome devil.

"The bones?" she repeated.

"I had a go at hazard last night at the Cocoa Tree. Me and George Stansbury. The devil was in the bones, so we both lost our blunt."

"You surprise me. You've learned the cant of the ton so readily."

"You're a good tutor." His gaze held her eyes captive while he murmured, "I only wish I could repay the favor."

She looked away. Why were her thoughts so all a-jumble? "The true test for you—" She stopped, unsure of what she meant to say. "The musicale next week. You'll meet Lord and Lady Kier-Windom." Marianne took a deep breath. "I hope

Georgie isn't encouraging you to be a gamester."

"I enjoy taking a chance now and again. Don't you?" he asked with a roguish smile.

"I don't believe in putting money at risk foolishly."

"Money wasn't what I had in mind."

Wolf took a step forward so that he stood looking down at her, his blue eyes sparking dangerously. When he leaned against the mantelpiece, his fingers came to rest within a breath of her cheek.

Did he mean her heart? "I don't risk what I don't wish to lose," she told him.

"Are you afraid? I'm surprised; I judged you to be more daring."

Marianne raised her chin defiantly, stung by the accusation. She certainly wasn't afraid of him. And she'd prove it.

"Who are you?" she demanded.

Wolf glanced toward the drawer of the desk. "Your question or Lord Brandon's?" he asked.

"What do you know of Lord Brandon?"

"More than you might imagine. George Stansbury told me about him, and he's the bloke who offered for you and you refused him. I'd pay no heed to Lord Brandon. Have you considered that the green-eyed monster might govern his words?"

"Lord Brandon jealous? Of *you?*" She hoped her laughter sounded more convincing to him than it did to her.

"I'm here in London with you," Wolf pointed out, "and he isn't. Might be enough to make a man jealous."

She retreated from the mantelpiece to stand in front of the shelves of books. When Wolf followed, her breathing quickened. Why, when she was near him, couldn't she think clearly?

To deflect him, she said, "The green-eyed monster. That's from Christopher Marlowe."

"No, you're mistaken. Shakespeare."

Again her suspicion of Wolf flared. "How are you able to quote the Bard?" she demanded.

He ignored her question. "Why do you keep running away from me like a startled deer?" Wolf asked.

"Why shouldn't I be wary? I don't know who you are or what you want. You claim to be a rustic from the wilderness of Canada; yet you quote Shakespeare, you learn our ways with uncommon ease, and you show an unusual interest in the Ramsdens. How can I help but be uneasy when it's possible you're an impostor."

"Have you ever spent a winter snowbound in a cabin with naught but a set of the classics, Shakespeare included, to keep you from going mad? I thought not. Well, I have. Besides, I've always had a good memory and a knack for aping others. The Ramsdens? I'm not interested in Harriet or any of the Ramsdens. Ever since the day I stood on the portico at Litchfield Hall and gazed down into the maze, all my thoughts have been of one person and one only." Wolf emphasized his final words by pointing at her. "And you are well aware of who that person is."

Marianne held up her hand to silence him, at the same time secretly wanting him to go on, to speak.

Even if his words later proved false, as he himself might prove false, she wanted to hear them. What was wrong with her? She must be halfway along the road to Bedlam.

Seeking a reprieve, she looked at Mrs. Featheringill, but the old woman sat sleeping in her chair. Walking quickly away from Wolf, she took Lucinda's quill from the rack on the desk and held it out to him.

"Today you're to practice your penmanship as well as your speech," she said breathlessly.

Shaking his head, Wolf reached for the quill, his fingers closing on both her hand and the pen. Why did his touch make her feel so weak, so vulnerable, and so elated? She pulled her hand from his, the quill falling unheeded to the carpet, and walked to the window, pulling the draped curtain to one side. She stared unseeingly at the square below.

She heard Wolf's footsteps come up behind her. "My only interest is in you," he said softly, "today and tomorrow and always. You and no other, never another."

She turned from the window and faced him. Drawing in her breath, she said as coolly as she could, "I realize, Mr. Clinton, you are rehearsing conversational gambits intended to intrigue young ladies just as you've been rehearsing the language of the ton. Don't you recall the suggestions in the improving books I loaned you?"

"'A gentleman must first consider his prospects in life,'" Wolf quoted from memory, "'and decide whether they justify his striving to win a lady's affections. He must study the likes and dislikes of the lady and adapt himself to them.' In Canada, we proceed in a different way."

"You're not in Canada, Mr. Clinton; you're in England."

"More's the pity, since in Canada we're more direct. When we know what we want, we go and take it if we can."

She felt a blush suffuse her face. "In Canada, in Canada, must you forever say 'in Canada'?" Looking into the depths of his blue eyes, she grew confused, uncertain. "Don't tell me again what they do in Canada," she said.

"I won't, instead I'll show you."

Wolf took her in his arms and drew her to him, his lips closing over hers in a tender, lingering kiss.

The room whirled around her, the bookshelves, the writing table, the fireplace, the curtained window, the square outside the window. All of London spun in giddy circles like a catherine wheel untl she was quite lightheaded.

For an instant—only for an instant, she reminded herself later—she returned his kiss. Then she pushed him from her, drawing in her breath with a gasp, and fled from the library. She heard Wolf call after her, but she paid him no heed, listening only to the pounding of her heart, its beat seeming to warn her over and over again, "Beware, beware, beware."

Chapter Eight

Marianne wrote the invitations to the musical evening to be held on the last Tuesday in May at the Hilton town house, her groom delivered them to the various London addresses, mostly in Mayfair, and by noon on Saturday the acceptances to what would be Wolf's first appearance in society lay neatly stacked on the writing table in the library.

Early on that Saturday afternoon, Marianne and Lucinda visited Miss Linwood's artistic exhibition at Saville House on Leicester Square. After paying their shilling admittance, they strolled leisurely around the crowded hall admiring the "canvases" in the display that had first opened seventeen years before in 1800. Miss Linwood wove colored wool into reproductions of famous works of art.

"Isn't that a perfectly lifelike portrait of Napolean?" Marianne asked. "And such an excellent copy of the original."

"Miss Linwood has been offered a thousand pounds for it," Lucinda told her. "And, according to George, three thousand for one of her larger works."

Marianne raised her eyebrows. "George? Not Georgie?"

Lucinda blushed. "He asked me to call him George. Everyone calls him Georgie, so he believes George sounds more personal. I hope I can remember."

Marianne smiled, happy for Lucinda. At last Georgie had shown the wit to appreciate her, and she was obviously attracted to that most amiable of men. If only, Marianne thought, she could read her own heart as easily. Wolf Clinton's kiss had spun her into a giddy whirl, one moment deciding to cancel the musical evening and have nothing to do with him, the next moment changing her mind, a few minutes later finding herself counting the days, no, not just the days, the hours, the very minutes until she would see him again.

All at once she realized Lucinda had been speaking. "I'm sorry," Marianne said, "I must have been wool gathering. What did you say?"

"I only wish her works were more original. Copies, no matter how faithful, can never be more than imitations. A certain spark is missing. Take Mr. Clinton, for instance. I wonder whether he can ever truly be a gentleman."

"He's not a copy," Marianne protested with a vehemence that surprised her. "To me he seems an original in every way."

"I wonder if he is," Lucinda murmured almost to herself as they completed their circuit of the display. She seemed about to go on; but when Marianne offered no encouragement, she said no more, and they made their way in silence through the crowd to their waiting carriage.

Once they were on their way, Lucinda asked, "Could we drive to the Thames and see the Waterloo Bridge?"

"Waterloo Bridge?" Marianne frowned until she remembered the name of the Strand Bridge had been changed. "Of course," she said.

Brabson stopped the carriage on the embankment above the Thames where they had an unobstructed view of the nearly completed bridge.

"It's beautiful," Marianne said. "The nine arches are like graceful leaps from here to the other side."

Although the massive stone structure was finished, workmen still toiled paving the broad and level roadway leading from the north to the south bank of the Thames.

"Georgie informs me—" Lucinda immediately corrected herself. "I meant to say George informs me his father will be one of those honored at the ceremonies when the bridge opens on the eighteenth of June."

Waterloo Bridge's opening would celebrate the second anniversary of the defeat of Napolean.

"I took note," Lucinda said, "of how you hesitated when I used the new name of the bridge. Believe me, I remark on this for a reason."

Marianne wasn't certain she wished to hear the reason if it had anything to do with Wolf. After asking Brabson to drive on, she said, "It's human nature to become accustomed to a name and resist a change. Georgie, for instance."

Lucinda said nothing for a time, finally murmuring, "I have a truly absurd notion."

From Lucinda's tone, Marianne knew her friend didn't consider her notion absurd at all but feared *she* might. Her curiosity piqued now, Marianne asked, "And just what is your notion?"

"It concerns Wolf Clinton."

As I suspected, Marianne thought. Yet she found herself wanting to talk about him. She was eager to hear his name, no matter what Lucinda had to say about him. In truth, it bothered her how often he was in her thoughts, but she didn't seem able to banish him.

"You're fearful," Marianne speculated, "that Wolf will commit a grievous blunder at our musicale, leading Lord and Lady Kier-Windom to expose him as a Canadian trapper."

"Nothing of the sort. Remember how you once suspected he might be playing an undergame?"

"I vaguely recall saying something of the sort."

"You said Wolf learned our ways too readily, he rarely mentioned his life in Canada, and had a strange interest in the Ramsdens. Oh, yes, and he found you so readily when you lost your way in the Litchfield maze."

All that was true, Marianne conceded to herself, and yet she no longer believed Wolf practiced deception. Ever since he kissed her, she had been secretly building dream castles in the air. If she allowed herself to distrust him now, those castles would tumble to the ground. And in so doing, break her heart.

A man she cared so much for could not be false to her. In a matter of this importance, her instincts could not betray her. The truth was simple and uncomplicated: Mr. Wolfson Clinton was what he claimed to be, no more and no less, and if Lucinda believed otherwise, her friend was sadly mistaken.

"Do you actually believe he plays an under-game?" Marianne asked, hard put to keep tartness from her voice.

"No, not exactly." Lucinda hesitated as though aware her suspicions might wound her bene-factress. "I told you my notion was absurd. I'm certain you'll agree it is."

"Don't let your suspicions fester like unlanced wounds. Tell me what they are."

"At times," Lucinda said, "when you or someone else unexpectedly says his name, Wolf hesitates just as you did when I mentioned the Waterloo Bridge. He seems unsure, as though his own name was new and unfamiliar to him."

"That's a slender thread to use to hang a man." Even as she defended him, Marianne admitted the truth of Lucinda's observation.

"Have you remarked," Lucinda went on, "how his speech wanders from proper English to what I imagine must be a Canadian dialect? I have the impression he's continually having to remind

113

himself how to speak."

"When learning what amounts to a new language, as Wolf is doing, you're apt to err now and again. I see nothing strange in that." The tartness broke through, edging her words.

Lucinda looked at her gravely. "Remember the day Mr. Clinton rescued Paul from that terrible Mr. Moles? Wolf said something then I didn't understand, and ever since I've been twisting and turning it as I might worry a stubborn knot in my embroidery floss."

Marianne closed her eyes as she tried to recall Wolf's words. "He mentioned being akin to Paul in some way," she said finally.

"Exactly. And, although he didn't say it in so many words, I had the distinct impression he meant Paul had been raised in a way that reminded him of his own upbringing."

"Obviously he wanted us to know he didn't come from a family of wealth and position."

"He could have meant that," Lucinda admitted. "Yet he sought to conceal the matter, and so I suspect there was more involved. In some way, I think he was hinting that he, too, was an orphan who had been raised by strangers."

Marianne drew herself up. Surely Lucinda could see she was displeased. It wasn't like her friend to persist in the face of displeasure.

"More and more this notion of your reminds me of one of your novels," Marianne snapped. "Your first, if I remember aright, the one still residing in the trunk in the attic. Wasn't the title *The MacDonald Inheritance?*"

"I don't mean to upset you," Lucinda said. "I did warn you my notion was absurd. Just because I once told an orphan's tale, though, doesn't mean there are no orphans or that Wolf isn't an orphan. Or like an orphan in some way."

"He's never claimed to be an orphan or not to be one. Perhaps he is; I'll ask him. I suspect you're doing your utmost to lead me somewhere unpleasant with this trail of hints, yet for the life of me I can't envision where."

The carriage clattered past the fenced park in the center of Cavendish Square. Amelia Willoughby, who lived next door to them, was leaving the park and locking the gate behind her.

"We're almost home," Lucinda said. "Come with me to the library so that I can read you a passage from a draft of my Ramsden novel. When you hear it, I think you'll understand and, perhaps, forgive me."

As soon as they were settled in the library, Lucinda at the writing desk and Marianne on the confidante, Lucinda leafed through a sheaf of papers until she found the one she wanted.

"Listen to this passage," Lucinda said. "In this draft I still use the Ramsden names.

"Frederic was sickly from birth," Lucinda read, "and on several occasions during his infancy his life flickered like a dying candle flame. He lived to suffer an illness-ridden childhood, becoming the coddled pet of his mother and the despair of a father who believed the twisted sapling called into question the vigor of the fathering oak.

"At least three consequences sprang from

115

Frederic's sickly childhood, and all were to have lasting effects on the Ramsdens. Firstly, young Frederic, inept at sports and games, became a voracious reader of mathematics, poetry, literature, and science, an activity little indulged in by any male Ramsden within memory. Secondly, his father, concerned for the boy's physical and moral fate, vowed to introduce him to manly pursuits at the first opportunity. And thirdly, the boy's physician, impressed by the earl's combination of elan and tact, introduced him to his older brother, who was the secretary for colonial affairs."

Lucinda went on to describe the journey to Canada and the canoeing accident in which the earl was drowned and Frederic was lost. When she put down the final page, Lucinda looked expectantly at Marianne.

"I know exactly what you're about to suggest," Marianne said, "and I don't for one moment believe it."

"I told you my notion was absurd," Lucinda said for perhaps the fourth time.

"Whenever I read a fiction and a character is lost at sea or in the jungle or in the confusion of a great battle and given up for dead, I always expect him to reappear in the final chapter. But that certainly doesn't mean it happens in real life."

"Wolf Clinton *could* be Frederic," Lucinda insisted. "He's the proper age, he does exhibit a great deal of book learning, he does come from Canada, and he is interested in the Ramsdens."

Marianne shook her head. "I suspect you believe the accident on the river caused him to lose his memory." When Lucinda nodded, Marianne went on, "And that he truly thinks he's Mr. Wolfson Clinton when in fact he's Frederic Ramsden, Ninth Earl of Litchfield."

"Exactly. He's been drawn against his will to London and Litchfield Hall by the same homing instinct that year after year induces birds to fly thousands of miles to their feeding grounds."

Marianne knew Lucinda often became enthralled by romantic imaginings, for how else could she create her fictions, but this time she had surpassed herself. Not only was the "absurd notion" precisely that, but the story had the power to cause great distress if carelessly circulated.

"You mustn't mention your notion to anyone," Marianne warned. "Harriet must not be reminded needlessly of her great loss, even after all these years. You should only tell her if you're certain, and of course you're not. How could you be?"

"There must be a method for discovering the truth. We might subtly inquire of Wolf about his upbringing."

Marianne frowned, wondering whether to tell Lucinda there was another, perhaps better way. With a sigh, she decided to speak. After all, there was a possibility, no matter how remote, that Lucinda could be right.

"There *is* the birthmark," she said.

Lucinda's eyebrows flew up. "A birthmark! I never heard of a birthmark."

"Harriet mentioned it to me several years ago. Frederic was born with a large red mark in the shape of a shield on his right shoulder. However, you can't possibly request Mr. Clinton to bare his upper torso to you."

The thought of a bared male torso caused Lucinda to blink, then flush in embarrassment. "Yet there must be a way," she said. "And if there is," she vowed, "I'll find it."

Chapter Nine

"A toast!" George cried, holding his glass aloft. "To the hot air balloon!"

Lord Brandon, disguised as Wolfson Clinton raised his own glass of Madeira, but his friend's exuberance, rather than buoying his own spirits, lowered them even further. "This is a hydrogen balloon, Georgie," he corrected. "All in all, a much safer craft."

"Whatever," George said, downing his wine and lowering his glass with a flourish. "And your ascension? When do you challenge the heavens?"

Lord Brandon did his best to inject enthusiasm into his words. "At a date of my choosing within the next eight weeks, the weather permitting. M. Delacroix promises to have the aerostat inflated and ready for flight on a mere six hours' notice."

"I envy you. If only I could join you in the sky."

"I'd like to have you with us, but it's impossible, I'm sorry to say. The basket carries only two, and even they must be of moderate heft—the gas in the

119

envelope will support no more—and Delacroix would agree to but one flight. In August he intends to cart the balloon north to Glasgow, where he'll solicit subscriptions for a publicly viewed ascension."

"Ah well, time's wasting," George said. "If I'm to glimpse this latest wonder of yours, we'd best be on our way."

They drove in George's phaeton, George exclaiming over the proposed flight, Lord Brandon attempting to match his friend's good spirits yet failing. George, noting Lord Brandon's tacturnity, proposed they refresh themselves at a public house, the Bull's Head, where Lord Brandon's disguise would excite no comment.

As soon as they were served, George held his mug of ale aloft. "To the general!" he proposed.

Lord Brandon joined the toast, conscious that the initial suspicious glances of the habitués of the Bull's Head had changed to warm smiles in a matter of minutes thanks to Georgie's encompassing good cheer. Everyone liked Georgie wherever he went, and Georgie liked everyone in turn.

Lord Brandon, while he would forgive Georgie anything, had never been able to bring himself to completely excuse the more grievous faults of a few of his acquaintances. He found Lord Kier-Windom to be patronizingly smug, and Jack Rodale, he was convinced, cheated at whist, although he'd never caught him red-handed, and the general. . . .

Yes, the general, Georgie's father. Hero of Waterloo he might be, yet did valor in battle grant him the right to attempt to browbeat his only son into following in his oversized bootprints?

Brooding over the general's blindness to his son's genuine charm suited Lord Brandon's mood, and he responded to his friend's sallies only in monosyllables.

When they were on their way again, rattling over a rutted road in the warehouse district on the north bank of the Thames, George said, "Talent! The general admires talent."

Lord Brandon grunted a noncommittal reply.

"After my mother passed on, God rest her soul," George said, "and following a decent interval, the general entered his musical period. My name for it, not his. Opera singers, dancers, even a harpist, by God."

"'If music be the food of love,'" Lord Brandon murmured, "'play on.'"

"Didn't resent it, not one bit," George said. "A man has to live his own life. I'm not one to judge. Don't be the first to throw stones, I say."

"You rarely pass judgement, Georgie. You like everyone."

George shook his head. "Don't care for pickpockets. Tell myself they need the blunt more than I do, though." George sighed. "'Why don't he have a talent?' What the general asks himself every time he sets eyes on me. If only I could sing exceedingly well. Or fence. Or shoot. Or be a pugilist. Or own the grandest collection of snuffboxes in all London. Even be a skilled billiard player. But what am I? No matter what I attempt, I'm fair to middling, no less, no more."

"Your father's badgering doesn't seem to have put you out of sorts."

"How could it? On such a day as this?"

The gathering twilight appeared perfectly ordinary to Lord Brandon. The sun had set, the vault of the moonless sky was still blue, a heavy, damp fetid odor emanated from the nearby river, and scuttling noises in the gutters hinted of rats.

"One reason comes to mind," Lord Brandon told him. "Come Monday you have to surrender this phaeton."

"I'll win it back within a fortnight."

"Tell me the secret of your happiness, Georgie. Is it amenable to being bottled and sold at profit? If so, I'll gladly purchase a dozen or two."

"It's love," George declared, grinning broadly. "Lucinda encourages my suit, so all's right with the world."

"You've discovered love, and we have arrived at our destination. Stop in front of that warehouse with the flagpole atop its roof." Lord Brandon couldn't help his sour tone. Love was the last thing he wished to be reminded of.

After George reined in and tethered the horses to a hitching post, Lord Brandon, taking a key from his pocket, led the way to the door of the large wooden structure.

A man's voice hailed them, and they turned to see the burly figure of the watchman approaching along the footpath with the rolling gait of a jacktar. "Ah, good evening to you, Mr. Clinton," he said.

"I intend to show my friend the balloon," Lord Brandon told him.

"The monseer's been and gone, he has," the watchman informed them.

"This is for your diligence, Mr. Hines." Lord Brandon spun him a coin, the watchman catching it with a swoop of his hand.

Giving Lord Brandon a salute, Hines said, "Give a hail if you be wanting me," before ambling off.

After unlocking the door, Lord Brandon followed George into the warehouse's single cavernous room. Since the row of windows near the rafters provided scant light, Lord Brandon removed a lantern from a peg near the door, lit the wick and, holding the lantern high in front of him, threaded his way between bales and crates to the far side of the room.

"I fear you'll be disappointed," he warned George. "There's precious little to see."

"'Tis the idea. That men can fly. Fabulous." George pointed to a huge pile of folded blue cloth. "The envelope?" he asked.

"Woven of linen and then varnished. When inflated, the balloon is thirty feet across."

"And this netting?"

"Mantles the top and sides of the envelope. This basket"—he indicated what appeared to be an oversized clothes basket some ten feet in diameter—"is fastened to the bottom of the net."

"Those poles? Must be forty feet long. And the barrels?"

"M. Delacroix implants the poles in the ground," Lord Brandon explained, "supporting them with wires tethered to stakes, and stretches another wire between the pole tops. He suspends the balloon from the midpoint of the wire during its inflation. The barrels hold the water, oil of vitriol and the iron parings, the mixture producing the hydrogen M. Delacroix inserts into the balloon by means of a long tube."

"Always thought balloons used hot air," George said. "Sort of a flying stove arrangement."

"There's those that swear by hot air, but the stoves are likely to set fire to the fabric and bring down the balloon in flames. Since M. Delacroix's brother nearly lost his life in such a fall, he now flies only in hydrogen aerostats."

"You're a lucky devil, Brandon. No one can accuse you of being a dry-boots."

"Wolf, not Brandon."

"Brandon, Wolf. My God, the confusion. Right enough, Wolf it is then, what luck to be able to make an ascension. Danger puts a nice edge to the flight, damme if it don't."

"M. Delacroix shuns unnecessary risk. The 'monseer' even disputes the name I've given the balloon, worries that I'm tempting fate. I call it 'Phaeton.'"

"Named the balloon for a carriage? Odd choice."

"Not for a carriage, for the Greek god Phaeton, son of Helios, the sun god. Legend has it that Phaeton borrowed his father's sun chariot. Alas,

124

he had heavy hands, and his steeds bolted, swooping so near the Earth he scorched a great portion of Africa, turned the area into the Sahara Desert. His father had to kill him with a thunderbolt before he wreaked more havoc. The name's even more fitting for this airborne chariot than for a mere carriage."

"Thank the Lord the general has no thunderbolts to hurl at me." George shook his head. "Your erudition bedazzles me. Strikes me dumb. You're a lucky man, must be sitting atop the world."

Lord Brandon shook his head, abruptly turning away from George and slamming his fist against a wooden pillar. He grimaced in pain.

"What's amiss?" George asked.

"I'm not on top of anything. I've been a fool," Lord Brandon said vehemently. "A simpleton, a nitwit, a goose, a scatterbrain, a rattlepate."

"Surely not all of those."

"All those and more. A dolt, a dunce, an addlepate."

George stared at his friend in consternation, for he'd never before heard him excoriate himself in such a way. Sick at heart because of Lord Brandon's evident distress, George stood mute. When Lord Brandon turned to him, though, his wan smile heartened George.

"Perhaps we should peruse my cellar book and then share a bottle of my best Madeira," Lord Brandon said, "while I relate my tale of how my miscalculation is leading to my ruination."

They left the warehouse, Lord Brandon locking

125

the door behind him. Stars now shone overhead, and the buildings across the roadway were bathed in a silver glow.

"The moon's rising," George said.

They followed the footway until, between two warehouses, they saw the full moon over the Thames, the light creating a shimmering path across the water. Drawn by the unearthly beauty of the scene, they descended stone steps to an embankment beside the gently lapping water of the river.

The two friends walked onto a small dock jutting into the Thames, crossing the timbers to the end of the quay, where they sat side by side staring in silent awe at the huge yellow orb of the moon silhouetting the six-hundred-year-old London Bridge.

Lord Brandon was first to speak. "Your monetary fortunes are at a low ebb, Georgie," he said, "yet you're elated because Lucinda favors your suit. In a few weeks' time, I'll make a balloon ascension, a thing I've long dreamed of, and yet I'm mired in melancholy. Because of Marianne. Is love so all-powerful it overshadows all else?"

"Does Marianne suspect your double game? Is she about to expose you?"

"No, neither, the cause of my distress is worse, much worse." Lord Brandon drew in a deep breath. "Far from suspecting me, she's utterly convinced Wolf Clinton's exactly who he claims to be. *And*"—he stressed the word—"she's proceeded to fall in love with him."

126

George was shocked. "She admitted as much?"

"No, no, not in words. She didn't have to; I can reaad her heart. I've been hoist by my own petard. My attempts to use Wolf's excessive ardor to drive her into Lord Brandon's arms have only succeeded in enamoring her of Wolf. What a damnably unexpected turn."

George pondered the problem. "Solution's obvious," he said at last. "Discard the beard. Reveal your true identity to Marianne. It's Brandon who's captured her heart, not Clinton. Dash it all, there is no Wolf Clinton, not on this side of the Channel."

"You don't understand women, Georgie. If I drop my disguise and confess all, Marianne will be hurt to the quick; she'll never forgive me. Never. She'll claim I tricked her, held her up to the ridicule of the ton. Claim it with some justification, I'm forced to admit."

"Because you love her, remember that."

"That's my only excuse, that I love her." Whenever he saw her, his doubts, his hesitation to assume responsibility, became as nothing. "Yet she sets great store by honesty, and I'll have shown myself, in her eyes, to be dishonest by courting her in the guise of a stranger."

"With the purest of motives."

"Women don't think as we do, Georgie; they view all our actions in the worst possible light. I must admit if someone practiced such a piece of gammon on me, I'd be more than a bit upset."

"You've convinced me," George said. "Your

plight's well-nigh hopeless." He took a shilling from his pocket and handed the coin to Lord Brandon.

"What's this for?"

"Luck. Your only chance. Toss the shilling over your left shoulder into the river. Worked for me at the Cocoa Tree more than once."

Lord Brandon half-turned and threw the coin. They heard a faint plop from the river below them.

"Marianne's musical evening is in three days' time," Lord Brandon said. "What am I to do, Georgie? If I follow my heart and make love to Marianne as Wolf Clinton, I muddy the puddle even more and worsen my plight. Yet if I show the least partiality to Rolissa Highsmith or Lillian Marsh, I'll bring down Marianne's wrath on my head."

"Ah, Rolissa. A ripe apple waiting to be plucked."

"True, Georgie." All at once Lord Brandon sprang to his feet, beaming happily. "I have it," he cried, "I have the answer. To think I've been staring the solution to my problem in the face all this time without seeing it."

"Rolissa?"

"Of course! Why didn't I think of her before? Rolissa Highsmith will prove to be my salvation."

Chapter Ten

The guests began arriving a few minutes before eight, the curricles, landaus, and assorted other carriages swinging grandly around Cavendish Square before stopping in front of the Hilton town house to deliver their fashionably attired occupants. The conveyances then proceeded to nearby Mortimer Street to wait until summoned for the drive home.

After Slater met the guests at the door, a footman escorted them to the sitting room by way of the foyer where, no matter how many times they had seen the room before, they invariably stopped to exclaim in admiration. The foyer was unparalleled, three stories high overtopped by a glassed dome. Built of imported variegated marble, the circular room represented grand extravagance. Water spouted from the mouth of a leaping marble fish at its center, cascading from one shallow basin to another until it reached the crystal-clear pool at the bottom, where goldfish swam serenely.

A marble balustrade girdled the second floor, and those passing by below, if they looked up, caught a glimpse of a small boy staring in awe from between the banisters. Paul, in his nightgown and robe, had never before seen the likes of these ladies and gentlemen of the ton.

Marianne, a velvet ribbon in her black hair and her grandmother's gold and pearl necklace about her neck, wore an elegantly cut dress of pale green crepe bound at the bodice with gold braid. She greeted her guests at the entrance to the sitting room, which had been expanded for the musicale by sliding open the doors to the adjacent drawing room.

Did they notice, she wondered, her heightened awareness, her glow of happiness? Though she endeavored to hide her excited anticipation of Wolf's arrival, her emotion was too great to conceal. Her guests must suspect her eagerness wasn't entirely due to looking forward to a musical evening in their company.

Smiling, curtsying, murmuring a few words, she welcomed them all: the marquis of Worcester, beaming and jovial, and his wife the marchioness, pale and timid, Henry Bone, the enameller, as smooth and polished as one of his creations, Viscount and Lady Castlereagh, as usual offering their gifts of gossip, tales of the profligate doings of the Prince Regent and his court, Sir George Beaumont, the artist, begging, as he did with flattering regularity, to be allowed to paint Marianne's portrait.

"Tonight," he told her, "you look especially lovely, like a reluctant bud of early spring at last bursting into bloom at the June sun's prompting."

He couldn't realize how close he came to describing exactly how she felt.

General Stansbury and George arrived escorting, surprisingly, Harriet Ramsden, her face aglow, her white satin gown almost modish.

"The general would not take no for an answer," she confided to Marianne. "I told him I never attended evening affairs? I warned him I had nothing to wear?" She leaned closer to whisper. "I dare not repeat what the general said to *that*."

Harriet and the general made an interesting couple, Marianne thought, however unlikely. It couldn't help but do Harriet good to enjoy a man's escort again. Marianne wished them well. Everyone should be as happy as she; no one should have to go through life alone.

And still they came, an earl, a viscount, a sculptor. Finally, in their own eyes fashionably late, Percy and Hannah Highsmith, Earl and Countess of Kier-Windom, accompanied by their daughter Rolissa, entered the crowded room. Lord Kier-Windom was a tall and balding man, his wife short and voluminous. The curvaceous Rolissa stood dimpled and smiling, her light brown hair piled high in a fashionable chignon with curls tied with red ribbon, the bow over her left eye. Her cheeks were delicately touched with Bloom of Ninon, and her red satin gown clung seductively, its neckline plunging in daring décolletage.

"Rolissa, you've never looked lovelier," Marianne said. Tonight her blissful goodwill extended even to Rolissa Highsmith.

For an instant Rolissa's hazel eyes met hers, and to her surprise, Marianne thought the younger woman raised a cynical eyebrow. Then Rolissa curtsied to acknowledge the compliment, revealing the dark valley between her breasts, and Marianne decided she must be mistaken. Rolissa hadn't the subtlety to be cynical.

At that moment Wolf Clinton made his appearance, elegant in black and white. Marianne turned to him, Rolissa's answering words of flattery unheard and unheeded. Wolf's arrival, even though expected, made her pulses race. When he raised her fingers to his lips, she blushed, imagining every eye was on them, their secret revealed.

She looked up at him, but Wolf didn't meet her gaze. In fact, he appeared tentative and ill-at-ease, his expression for all the world that of a child discovered at mischief. She frowned; something was obviously amiss.

Perhaps Canadians were altogether different from Englishmen. Could it be that to these colonials a kiss meant nothing, promised nothing, pledged nothing? Could they be so callous? She knew so little of Canadians and particularly so little of Wolf Clinton. Yet she had been certain on the fateful day in the library when he held her in his arms that he admired her, cared for her and, yes, wanted to marry her. Now, she sensed, their affinity had suffered a sea change but not into something rich and strange.

"Who is that delightful creature?" Wolf's gaze followed Rolissa's retreating form.

Marianne fought back her anger. He was goading her, much as he'd done on the walkway outside the tailor shop. She'd thought he'd have no more need to jab and feint as if they were pugilists testing one another's defenses. For her, their kiss had changed the world. Apparently Wolf felt differently. Had their kiss meant so little to him?

"The young lady in question," she said stiffly, "is Miss Rolissa Highsmith. You'll soon have the pleasure of hearing her play the piano and, if you're extremely fortunate, sing as well."

"I'm sure she'll charm us all," Wolf said, still not meeting her gaze.

Hurt and disappointed, she was about to tell him to speak for himself when Lucinda appeared at Wolf's elbow and led him into the room to meet Lord and Lady Kier-Windom. From the corner of her eye, Marianne watched as he was introduced, and glimpsed him talking easily to both of them. After a few minutes, Lady Kier-Windom used her fan to unobtrusively beckon her daughter to join them.

It was time, high time, Marianne decided, to begin the musicale.

When Marianne entered the room, the guests took their places on the cream-colored chairs upholstered in maroon plush, a few of the gentlemen stood near the fireplace, while old Mrs.

Featheringill, hands clasped in her lap, watched from her chair in the far corner of the drawing room.

Rolissa walked to the pianoforte, an Erard, where she sat demurely on the chair with her back properly straight and her hands poised stiffly above the keys. She played selections from Mozart with faultless, if mechanical, precision, and when she finished, the applause was generous, especially from the gentlemen.

Amanda Withers, tall and extraordinarily thin, came to stand beside the pianoforte, singing a joyous ballad to Rolissa's accompaniment:

O farewell grief and welcome joy
Ten thousand times therefore,
For now I have found mine own true love
Whom I thought I should never see more.

She next sang the tragic tale of Barbara Allen:

All in the merry month of May,
When green buds they are swelling
Young Jimmy Green on his death bed lay
For the love of Barbara Allen.

To her dismay, Marianne felt tears smart in her eyes. Blinking the away, she glanced around her to see if anyone had noticed, but all eyes were on Amanda. And, in Wolf's case, on Rolissa.

I don't care, Marianne told herself. *He's proved he's not worth caring about.*

Finally, for the *piece de resistance,* she introduced Calivari, the Italian tenor. Since Calivari's appearance had not been announced, and because he had insisted on waiting in the morning room until the time arrived for his performance, his name was greeted with gasps of pleased surprise and a ripple of excited comment.

Despite her low spirits, Marianne felt a little frisson of satisfaction when she overheard Lord Castlereagh remark to his wife, "You can always expect the delightfully unexpected at one of Miss Hilton's musicales."

Calivari, a darkly handsome Neapolitan of middle years with generous sideburns and thick black hair curling to his collar, held up his hands for quiet.

"I will sing selections," he said in accented English, "from a new opera by Gioachino Rossini, a talented young countryman of mine. He calls the work *Almaviva*, but you may be familiar with the story as *The Barber of Seville*. Almaviva is a young nobleman who assumes many disguises, as a troubador named Lindero, as a guardsman and as a music teacher, all to win the heart of his true love, the beautiful Rosina."

A nobleman in the guise of a commoner, Marianne thought, *just the opposite of Wolf Clinton, a commoner disguised as a gentleman. And common is certainly the correct word for his behavior. I expected better of him, I expected*—no, she wouldn't dwell on her disappointment.

"I will sing a song from the opera," Calivari told them. "Almaviva is serenading his beloved from the street beneath her window, telling her the dawn is breaking and asking her to give him but a single smile."

When Calivari sang, the warmth and richness of his voice held all enthralled. Except, Marianne saw, for Wolf, whose gaze remained on Rolissa. Marianne turned away, suddenly unable to bear one more moment of his indifference to her.

Slipping from the room, she rounded the foyer on her way to the kitchens to be certain, she told herself, that Slater was prepared to oversee the serving of the punch, canapes, and hors d'oeuvres as soon as the music ended. All the while she knew full well she had left because of Wolfson Clinton. Let him make a fool of himself over Rolissa; she had no intention of watching him do it.

Through the open door of the morning room she noticed a tall free-standing black and gold Chinese screen near the window on the far side of the room. Who had brought the screen here from the box room and for what purpose? she wondered, intending to ask Slater. The muted lilt of the music, though, followed her all the way to the kitchens, the tender words of love falling bittersweet on her ears, and by the time she found Slater, she had forgotten about the screen.

Marianne returned to the sitting room in time for Calivari's encore. She joined the storm of applause, watching her guests swarm around the beaming Italian tenor, then saw George Stansbury leave Lucinda's side and hurry to the two enormous cut-glass punch bowls at the rear of the drawing room.

George sampled the punch. When Marianne

136

joined him, he said, "Happen to be something of an authority on punch. Quite the thing, this."

"The recipe is yours," she told him. "Large lemons pared thin, a generous portion of French brandy—"

"Good, good, only French will do. Add a syrup of the best sugar boiled in spring water—"

"Pour in warm milk stirred with the rinds of the lemons, and there you have it."

"No, within an ace but not quite. Let the mixture stand three days. Shake well on occasion. Then filter through paper. Result: delicious. You must sample a glass, Miss Marianne."

Though intending to refuse, she suddenly changed her mind. "Perhaps I will," she said, accepting the glass.

"Not all in one swallow. You must savor it."

She ignored him. "Pray refill my glass, Georgie."

He stared at her, perplexed. "A bit aflutter," he asked kindly, "the musical evening and all?" When Marianne shook her head, he said, "Calivari was an inspiration." She said nothing, so George hastened to assure her, "Wolf's scored a hit, a palpable hit."

"At least with one guest, as everyone must be aware." She glanced to where Wolf stood leaning over the seated Rolissa, talking earnestly.

She thought George reddened. Why in heaven's name? she asked herself.

George shifted uneasily from foot to foot. "Don't worry," he told her. "All's for the best. Be patient, you'll see. You have my word."

"Georgie," she said, puzzled, "I don't have the least notion what you're talking about."

"Probably you think Wolf's only constant in his inconstancy."

She remembered saying similar words to Lord Brandon. "That's Swift," she told George.

"Swift? Don't follow you, sorry. Is that the name for the new slang?"

"No, Jonathan Swift, the author." George always managed to make her stray from the subject at hand. "What are you trying to tell me, Georgie?" she asked.

"Can't say more. Lips sealed. Said too much as it is. Have to bring this"—he held up a glass of punch—"to Lucy. Quite insistent, she was. Never knew she had such a craving for punch. Wonderful girl, Lucy," he added. "Keen mind. Quick wit. Understands a person."

"Take her the punch, Georgie."

Ah, men, Marianne thought as she watched George make his way to Lucinda's side, thinking only of themselves, standing up for each other no matter what. Lucinda must have followed her advice and praised George unreservedly, thus making her an understanding woman in his eyes.

Is that what she, Marianne, should do with Wolf Clinton? No, she couldn't bring herself to follow her own advice. If she meant so little to Mr. Clinton that he seized the very first opportunity to make himself agreeable to another woman, and Rolissa of all people, she'd have nothing more to do with him. The pain, she assured herself, would lessen in time.

With the taste of ashes in her mouth, she idly watched George proffer the glass of punch to Lucinda. And then she witnessed the most amazing accident. Lucinda, after nodding her thanks to George, rose to her feet and walked directly to where Wolf stood. As she neared him, Lucinda, the least awkward of women, appeared to trip, flinging the punch onto the back of Wolf's tailcoat.

Uttering profuse apologies, Lucinda took Wolf by the arm and led him to the door where Slater stood. Wolf, looking over his shoulder to examine and assess the damage—a large dark stain— protested when Slater urged him to go with him. At last Wolf gave in and followed the butler into the foyer.

By this time Lucinda was nowhere in sight.

Marianne suspected that Lucinda had spilled the punch on Wolf deliberately. Why? Out of loyalty to her, to interrupt his tête-à-tête with Rolissa? She quickly dismissed the idea. No, the incident must have been an accident. Or was it? Perhaps Lucinda wanted an excuse to talk to Wolf in private. As she was about to seek out Lucinda to discover the truth of the matter, Hannah Highsmith loomed in front of her.

"A most charming gentleman, your Mr. Clinton," Hannah gushed, "a most charming gentleman." Hannah habitually repeated her remarks as though to give herself and all others within earshot the opportunity to admire them anew. "Recently of Kingston in Jamaica, he informed us."

Marianne had no choice but to reinforce the tale she and Wolf had agreed on, all the while wondering where Lucinda and Wolf were at that moment. . . .

Wolf sat slumped in a chair in the morning room. Slater had taken both his tailcoat and his single-breasted waistcoat into the nether regions of the town house to be cleaned and dried, but he still wore his white linen shirt which, fortunately, had escaped the onslaught of Lucinda's punch.

Given this unexpected time for reflection, Wolf shifted uncomfortably in his chair. He despised what he was doing. The hurt in Marianne's eyes, the speaking way she had looked at him when he showed interest in Rolissa, had wounded him more than he could have imagined possible. His present course of action was both contemptible and dishonorable.

What else, though, could he do? He must make Marianne realize that Lord Brandon, not Wolf Clinton, was the man for her. How could she ever imagine she could find happiness in marriage—he strongly suspected a mirage of marriage to Wolf shimmered somewhere in her mind—with a Canadian fur merchant? Had she completely taken leave of her senses? Women indulged in some strange fancies, acted capriciously more often than not, but this was more than too much. Marianne living in the Canadian wilds? Impossible!

At least he could console himself in the

knowledge that what he was doing was for the best. Best for himself and, more importantly, of course, best for Marianne. The time was fast approaching for Lord Brandon's return from Bath to Marianne Hilton's welcoming embrace, figurative if not literal. The constancy of Lord Brandon's love would be akin to a warm spring breeze sweeping away the cold ingratitude and infidelity of Mr. Wolfson Clinton. Convinced by this review of the situation and fortified by his sense of righteousness, Wolf drew in a deep cleansing breath and sat straighter in his chair.

A slight noise roused him from his meditations.

His glance darted from the closed door leading to the foyer to the window. The sound had come from neither. Had he imagined it? No, someone or something was in the room with him. A cat, perhaps? Marianne kept several.

Wolf looked more closely at the tall Chinese triptych screen on the far side of the room. He drew in his breath. Two silver slippers peeked from beneath the screen, slippers most assuredly attached to a pair of female feet.

Who could be spying on him? And for what possible purpose? His initial inclination was to cross the room, pick up the screen and set it aside, revealing the interloper. Starting to rise, he hesitated, realizing he'd assumed Marianne was behind the screen but recalling that her slippers matched the green of her gown. Nor could it be Rolissa. He'd left her in the sitting room surrounded by admirers grateful for his unexpected baptism of punch.

141

Lucinda? Her slippers *were* silver, he recalled. A suspicion struck him unawares: She'd spilled the punch in order to bring him here to the morning room. What devious game was she playing? Had she gotten wind of his deception? By God, he'd soon find out.

He was on his feet when the door to the morning room opened and Slater bustled in carrying the waistcoat and tailcoat over one arm. After showing Wolf how successful his ministrations had been, Slater helped him into the coats.

Thanking him, Wolf waited until the butler left the room before turning once more to the screen.

"Wolf! Dash it all, I've searched high and low for you." George came in and clapped a hand on Wolf's shoulder.

Wolf turned and led his friend back into the foyer, closing the door behind them before drawing George to one side. "Lucinda Beattie's in the morning room"—he indicated the door with a nod—"concealed behind that Chinese screen."

"Lucinda? Hiding? What on earth for?"

"I haven't the foggiest. Perhaps you should find out while I go in search of the fair Rolissa."

George started to question him, but before he could speak, Wolf walked off. Frowning, George opened the morning room door and saw the black and gold screen. From where he stood, there was no sign of anyone concealed behind it. Was this some sort of hum of Wolf's?

He walked to the screen and craned his head around the near end.

Lucinda screamed.

"Only me," George told her. "Good God, Lucy, why are you hiding here?"

Lucinda turned several shades of scarlet. "To see his birthmark," she confessed.

"Birthmark? What birthmark? Whose birthmark?"

"Mr. Wolfson Clinton's birthmark, of course. But I couldn't see it; he wore his shirt the entire time he was in the room."

"I should hope so. With a woman here with him. Even though hidden."

"George, I should have confided in you long before this. You must brace yourself for a shocking revelation. Mr. Wolfson Clinton is not who you think he is."

George stared openmouthed. The game was up; Lucy had discovered Lord Brandon's secret, penetrated his disguise. But what the devil was this talk of a birthmark?

"Who is he?" George asked.

"Mr. Clinton is actually Frederic Ramsden," Lucinda told him. "But he doesn't know it."

"Frederic Ramsden? Doesn't know it?" George was completely nonplused. "Harriet's son? Returned from the dead?" Incredible! he thought. Lucinda had taken leave of her senses. Could the punch be to blame? "Let me sit," he said. "Head's in a whirl."

"I'll tell you all," Lucinda said. "And after I finish, there's something you must promise me you'll do so that the truth will at last be known and

143

all the loved ones reunited." She lowered her voice to a whisper. . . .

Rolissa Highsmith, having made good her escape from her bevy of persistent beaus in the sitting room, scanned the titles of the leather-bound volumes on the shelves of the Hilton library. Sliding one from its place, she slowly turned its pages, fondly remembering the many childhood hours she had spent poring over her copy of this very book.

If someone had entered the library at that moment, Rolissa would have quickly replaced the volume on the shelf and, if asked what book had so held her interest, would have replied without hesitation, "A romance by Miss Radcliffe." This, of course, would have been an unabashed lie.

The book in question actually bore the title, *An Introduction to Euclidean Geometry*, the author one Professor Noah Wallace. As a child, Rolissa had early demonstrated a marked proficiency in mathematics, had been fascinated by the logical proofs of plane geometry, and since ability, interest, and pleasure in a subject usually walked hand in hand, the *Introduction* became one of her favorites.

Rolissa's unexpected skill not only surprised her parents, but it dismayed them. To what possible use could a young gentlewoman put an adeptness at adding, subtracting, multiplying, and dividing? Mathematically inclined men might seek employment in counting houses or, *in extremis*, as moneylenders or bookmakers, and women of a lesser station might use the ability to teach others who would in turn teach others in a never-ending chain, but for Rolissa Highsmith an interest in mathematics could only distract her from a more practical and higher calling—the preparation for a suitable marriage.

Her tutors, therefore, were told to immediately discontinue Rolissa's instruction in the science of numbers, substituting other more beneficent subjects, and now the only remnants of her youthful indiscretion were a lingering nostalgia for geometry and an uncommon and often remarked-upon proficiency at the game of whist.

The forced redirection of Rolissa's education produced another, completely unexpected result. While she dutifully learned feminine skills, she at the same time developed a disdain for those skills and for the young women who so assiduously sought to perfect them.

There was one exception to her disdain; Rolissa grudgingly admired Marianne Hilton, thinking her several shades different from the other young women of her acquaintance. At times she wished she could speak freely and frankly to Marianne, could share her secret life with her as she had never been able to share it with other girls or with her mother, but the appropriate occasion never seemed to arise.

Because of her scorn for the ways of young women, Rolissa had no qualms about stealing their beaus by fair means or foul. More often than not, the theft proved ridiculously easy. Her comeliness combined with her ease of manner made her attractive to many, even to the most reserved and shy young men, while her knack of appearing ready to step over the line, without ever actually doing so, prompted the more dashing blades to pay her court.

Rolissa encouraged the attention of all of her many admirers because she feared that if the field dwindled to two or three, her mother would force her to make a choice among them, and this she did not want to do. She had never been in love and, having recently attained the age of eighteen, never expected to be. In her heart of hearts she believed herself destined to become a spinster, and she accepted that fate willingly. Perhaps then she could shape her life to her preferences rather than those of her mother.

For a moment when she first spied Mr. Wolfson Clinton, her heart had leapt, but after a few minutes of conversation with him she knew he was not a man destined to change her self-ordained fate. So now, when the door opened and Wolf entered the library, she was neither surprised nor elated nor disappointed.

"Ah, Mr. Clinton," she said in her flirtatious way, "you must be interested in good books."

"A smile from you would be worth all the words in all the books ever written," he told her. The music that had accompanied him into the room swirled about them. "I never learned to waltz," he said. "I thought you might teach me."

Smiling, Rolissa held out her arms. Wolf placed one hand in hers, the other about her waist, and before she had a chance to stop him, even if she had been so inclined, he drew her to him and kissed her.

She heard a gasp. Breaking away from Wolf and looking beyond him to the partly open door, she saw a flick of color, of green. Before she could see who it was, the door slammed shut. . . .

Marianne stumbled to the fountain in the center of the foyer, her thoughts in a jumble. She put her hand to her mouth, feeling nauseated. The same room. Wolf kissed Rolissa in the same room where he had kissed her. How could he be so cruel? So unfeeling? She hated him, hated Rolissa.

Walking to the far side of the foyer so that the fountain was between herself and the library door, she sat on the low marble wall that circled the pool. When she glanced quickly over her head, she wasn't surprised that Paul no longer peered from between the banisters. The boy must have tired of watching and listening and gone to bed.

In the pool beside her, the goldfish swam languidly to and fro. How placid they looked! If only life could be the same, with no responsibilities, no unfulfilled expectations, no dashed dreams.

A tear trickled down her cheek and fell into the water, creating a miniscule rippling circle. A murmur of conversation came from the sitting room as the waltz ended. Just as her hopes had ended.

She would *not* pity herself! Marianne dabbed

away her tears, put her hand in the pool and roiled the water, making the goldfish dart away from her.

Standing, she was on her way back to the sitting room and her momentarily forgotten guests when she heard the pianoforte and recognized the tune as "Barbara Allen." The melody rose clear and haunting, yet every so often the pianist struck a wrong note, jarring her. Who could be playing? she wondered.

From the doorway she saw a raptly attentive Calivari standing beside the pianoforte, but she could not see the pianist. When she approached Calivari, he turned to her and raised his hands in wonderment.

"Magnificent!" he cried. "Imagine, he has never played before. Remarkable! A prodigy! Another Mozart! He must receive instruction."

Two pillows had been placed on the piano chair, and on top of them Paul perched, looking tiny in his robe, ignoring Calivari, ignoring her, mindful only of the spell of the music his hands brought forth.

Chapter Eleven

Some time after midnight on his last day on the planet Earth, Mr. Wolfson Clinton strolled along Bond Street on his way to his lodgings. The pale glow of the gaslights on both sides of the street and the wisps of fog drifting above his head gave a semblance of otherworldliness to the London night.

Wolf paused outside a shuttered pastry shop where only the day before he had lingered over coffee. In all likelihood he would never eat there again. Across the street two dandies, boon companions after three bottles, staggered homeward with their arms about one another's shoulders, singing endless verses of a ribald ballad.

"Vanity of vanities, saith the Preacher, vanity of vanities; all is vanity."

The words from Proverbs came unbidden to his mind. Wolf wondered if he, as Lord Brandon, would ever again carouse the nights away with Georgie, Chichester, Boynton and all the others.

Probably he would; yet it would never seem the same again. His brief sojourn as Wolfson Clinton had forced him to view Lord Brandon's world differently, as from the peak of a lofty mountain, and that world had appeared small and unimportant and trivial.

He rat-a-tatted his walking cane on the railings of an iron fence, the faint echo speaking to him of loneliness. He'd miss his old life, but it was behind him now. He'd even miss Wolf Clinton. He vowed to let him pass from the London scene with the dignity he deserved. The next afternoon—wrong, it was now well past midnight, and so it would be that very afternoon—he'd see Marianne for the last time. As Wolf Clinton.

Only after promising to explain his boorishness at the musicale, only after telling her he intended to leave London and so she would never see him again, had she reluctantly consented to drive with him in Hyde Park.

What would he tell her? He didn't know. He intended somehow to inter Wolf once and for all while leaving him with some shreds of self-respect. At the same time he meant to prepare the way for the reappearance of Lord Brandon. So far he didn't have a ghost of an idea how to accomplish all this, but he was confident he would think of something when the time came. His wit would see him out of this tight corner as it had so often in the past.

He stopped directly across the street from the temporary lodgings he had leased as Wolfson Clinton. The rooms were small and crowded with bric-a-brac; he wouldn't miss them. Nor would he miss the ugly twin pillars flanking the oak door, the fanlight above, the small courtyard with its solitary, sparsely leafed tree and straggling shrubbery guarded by an iron fence with a creaking gate.

What was that? Had his tired eyes deceived him or did the dark figure of a man lurk behind the shrubs on the far side of the fence in front of his lodgings? A footpad? In this part of town at this hour of the night? Unlikely, yet anything was possible these days.

Wolf tightened his grip on his cane. He didn't intend to allow a lurking stranger to force him to seek help, nor was he about to go around the block and rouse a servant to let him enter by way of the rear door. Forewarned, he could handily deal with the most menacing blackguard the nether regions of London might spew forth.

Tilting his hat at a rakish angle, Wolf tucked his cane under one arm and flexed his gloved fingers. Taking the cane in hand once more, he strolled to the flagstone crossway, whistling "Barbara Allen" slightly off-key.

The tune recalled young Paul's performance. What a wonder the boy was at the pianoforte! Wolf debated whether to tell Georgie about his suspicions concerning the boy's parentage. No time to dwell on that filthy puddle now; he had a footpad to dispatch first.

To reach the door to his lodgings, Wolf would have to pass the bushes where the prowler waited and climb three steps. Although this would put his enemy behind him, the prowler would be forced to go through the gate and then climb the steps if he meant to attack Wolf while he paused to open the door. If this was indeed the man's intent, he faced an unpleasant surprise.

As Wolf walked past the fence, he saw, from the corner of his eye, a dark form crouched behind the privets. Wolf climbed the three steps, hearing footfalls behind him. A clumsy footpad, indeed. When the gate creaked, Wolf whirled around, his cane held ready to strike. The attacker, a cap drawn low on his brow, raised a cudgel above his head.

Wolf, about to hit the man over his left ear, held and stared in growing disbelief. The other man held at the same time. After a long pause, the man dropped his club and pulled off his cap.

"Georgie!" Wolf cried, unable to believe his eyes. "What the hell are you about?"

"Couldn't go through with it," George told him. "Didn't think I could. Couldn't."

"Go through with what? What brings you here in the small hours wielding a cudgel?"

"Promised Lucy," George said abashedly. "She asked me to and I promised."

"Why in God's name? Are you both mad?" Wolf shook his head. "Come in for a glass of Madeira, Georgie, and tell me what possessed that female scribbler to want me laid low. And why you agreed. Leave your club at the door, if you please."

"An old walking stick of my father's, actually," George said as he leaned it against the railing.

They went into the parlor of Wolf's lodgings, where, after lighting a lamp, Wolf handed his friend the promised glass of wine.

"Now," Wolf said after they settled themselves

in chairs drawn up in front of the cold fireplace, "tell me why I found you skulking in the bushes."

"Because of the birthmark," George explained. "Had to find out if you have a birthmark. In the shape of a shield. On your shoulder, can't recall which one. The reason Lucy hid behind the Chinese screen. To see your birthmark."

"I don't have a birthmark on either shoulder or anywhere else. Why did you think I might?"

"Ramsden had one," George told him. "Young Frederic Ramsden. Lucy has this notion Wolf Clinton is Frederic Ramsden. Chap didn't drown in Canada after all. I mean he did, but it's her idea he didn't."

"Good God, what an imagination that woman has." He frowned. "But Georgie, you know I'm Lord Brandon and not Wolf Clinton. How could *I* have the birthmark?"

"Remember what you told me?" George sounded plaintive. "Said when you wore the beard and all, when you were disguised as Wolf, you *were* Wolf. Told me to think of you as Wolf, act as if you were Wolf, not Lord Brandon. So if you were Wolf, how did I know you had no birthmark?"

"George! That won't do, that won't do at all. That's a harebrained excuse."

"Sorry. Didn't intend to hit you hard with the walking stick. Couldn't bring myself to it at all, you know. Regretted promising Lucy."

"If you insist on taking promises so much to heart, you should be wary of making them."

"I will. I give you my word I will, Wolf. Or Brandon. Or whatever. Had another reason for using the cudgel on you. Lucy's idea, really. She thought you'd forgotten you were Frederic Ramsden. Happened when the canoe capsized. A good knock on the head might bring back your memory."

"This is more than too much, Georgie. I don't want to hear another word about the birthmark. Tell Miss Beattie to confine her goose-brained romantic ideas to her novels." What wild notions would the woman come up with next? He wondered what story she'd concoct to explain his departure to Marianne.

"Will you do me a favor, Wolf?" George said. "Show me you don't have a—a you know what I mean. Don't scowl. Think on it. If I see you don't have one, I can truthfully tell Lucy you don't, and she'll forget the matter for all time."

"Probably you're right. Otherwise there's no telling what that woman might do next. None of us are safe." Wolf removed his tailcoat, waistcoat and shirt. "As you can see," he said, "I don't possess the least trace of a birthmark."

"Didn't think you did. All Lucy's idea. Mustn't blame her, though, have to be fair. Has to think like that or couldn't be a scribbler, could she?" George tried desperately to come up with a way to mollify his friend. "Marianne's a deep one," he said at last.

Wolf finished dressing and refilled their glasses before he asked, "In what way?" He recognized the ploy and, because he could never stay vexed with Georgie for long, went along with it.

"Erudite. I thought she'd heard some new slang.

To teach you, Wolf. She meant Jonathan Swift all the time."

"I don't follow you, Georgie."

"'I'm only constant in my inconstancy.' Jonathan Swift said it first. Or wrote it. I thought *you* did. Or the general. I forget which."

Wolf vaguely recalled hearing the epigram from Marianne. Mention of the general, however, recalled another matter.

"This is my last day as Wolf Clinton," he told George, touching his black beard. "I bid my *adieu* to Miss Marianne this afternoon."

"I liked Wolf. I'll miss him. Did cause all of us a spot of trouble, though."

"I want to be certain the climbing boy, Paul, is provided for before I take my leave," Wolf said. "I like the lad; I feel responsible for him. Marianne shouldn't have to shoulder his entire care and upbringing if at least one of his parents can be found."

"Parents? Has no parents. Lad's an orphan. That's the reason he was apprenticed as a climbing boy, you know."

Wolf regarded his friend. How should he put it? Straight from the shoulder was the only way likely to get across to Georgie, yet he could hardly just come out with it. He'd have to prepare the ground as best he could.

"This is a delicate matter, Georgie," he said, "yet one which we must face." He paused. "As you know, I've always considered you a gentleman, a man of experience, a man of the world."

"Hardly all that," George said modestly.

"And a man who does what is right no matter how personally painful it might be."

George's eyebrows flew up. "Surely you don't suspect the lad's mine? Why, I was only a boy myself when he was born. Hardly a precocious boy, either."

"Of course I don't think he's yours, Georgie. Let me go directly to the nub of the matter. The lad may very well be a by-blow of the general's." He waited to give George time to assimilate this. "I consider it your duty to face your father with the facts so he'll do the right thing."

George stared at Wolf, speechless.

"You yourself," Wolf went on, "mentioned to me the general's 'musical period' as you termed it. And I know for a fact, since the midwife in question later became one of our maids at Scarborough Hall, that a child was born at that very time, a child for whom the general paid all expenses."

"I seem to remember tittle-tattle along those lines," George admitted.

"The mother left England without taking the child with her, a mother who happened to be a talented pianist from Vienna. Don't you see, Georgie, Paul didn't come by his musical talent through pure chance. It came from his mother."

"I'd say your case is a Scottish 'not proven,' for all that."

"I didn't claim my surmise was a certain, only a possibility. Even if it's not probable but only possible, the question should be resolved one way or the other now. And you are the man to do it."

"Dash it all, Wolf, I don't know. The general and I are at swords' point as it is. The boy might be the straw to break the camel's back. Let me mull it over."

"I can't ask more of you, Georgie. I know in the end you'll do whatever's right and proper. I can always count on you for that."

Wolf sighed and passed his hand over his tired eyes. "Lord Brandon is about to depart Bath and return to London," he said. "With his arrival the skies will begin to clear." Wolf managed a smile. "A new day's dawning for me, for Marianne, for you, Georgie, for all of us. The worst is behind us, you just mark my words."

The June day sparkled. In Hyde Park, nannies gossiped across their prams, small children gamboled on the grassy slopes, boys and girls chased rolling hoops, couples courted while promenading and drinking ices, and old men sat side by side on benches and reminisced of the days of George II. They came to the Park by the hundreds, of all ages, from all stations in life, to see and be seen.

The southerly breeze brought an intoxicating warmth, a promise that this would be the best of summers. Frowns gave way to smiles; scowls became grins. Hats were tipped with an added flourish. Boys whistled, girls hummed, lovers picnicked beneath the fresh greenery of the trees, and would-be lovers daydreamed while reading romantic poems.

In all the great park only two people, a young

man and a young woman, Wolf Clinton and Marianne Hilton, seemed unaware of the glory of the day. Wolf, hunched in upon himself, drove his hired curricle along a shaded roadway with Marianne, stiff and distant, beside him.

"I desire your advice," Wolf said.

She didn't answer. *Being here is a mistake,* she told herself. *I should never have agreed to see him again. Why did I? Out of curiosity? Because of a forlorn hope that he might be able to explain himself? Why is it when I'm with him I feel as unsteady as a house of cards, ready to collapse at the slightest tremor, the least whisper?*

"First let me explain my charade with Rolissa Highsmith," Wolf said when Marianne remained silent. "What I did was because of you, for you."

For me? Marianne thought. *He made a fool of himself over Rolissa for me? How can I believe him? I should demand that he stop the curricle immediately so I can dismount and walk away. I never should have allowed myself to be persuaded into this folly.*

Yet she said nothing, watching the passing carriages, nodding whenever she recognized someone, holding herself aloof from Wolf and his unconvincing protestations of innocence.

"Another matter," he went on. "Your probably thought I learned the ways of the ton too readily. I fear I exaggerated my rusticity because I wanted to know you better. It was all a mistake, although, I hope and pray, not an unpardonable one."

"The mistake was mine as well as yours," Marianne told him tartly.

158

"About Miss Highsmith," Wolf said. "Rolissa. I wanted you to hate me, so I feigned being caught in her web. Rolissa means nothing to me. My apparent infatuation was a ploy I attempted, because to reveal my true circumstances was too painful."

"I no longer believe a word you tell me." She spoke as calmly as she could, struggling to keep emotion from her voice. "Use your ploys and your ruses on others. Please."

"I admit I deceived you. In more ways than I've admitted." Wolf sighed. "I'm having a damnable time saying this; my words are muddled; I'm making a proper hash of it." He snapped the whip, and the two bays broke into a trot. "The truth of the matter is I'm married."

Aghast, Marianne stared at him. Wolf a married man? He couldn't mean what he said; surely he was up to another of his tricks. It wasn't possible he had deceived her so cruelly. Her gloved hands clenched into fists.

"I can't credit what you're saying," she managed to tell him.

"I have no excuse for what I did," Wolf admitted. "Reasons, perhaps, but no excuses. Pray let me explain, though no explanation can atone for my transgression against your honor."

Wolf paused but then spoke again before she had a chance to answer. "I married when I was young," he said, "when I was only eighteen. Her name was, and is, Alfaretta. The first time I saw her, she'd been picking wild flowers; I'll always remember her like that, even after what happened later, running toward me across a field of yellow and white daisies."

Wolf shook his head. "My bride didn't know about the taint in her blood; her mother never warned her, never warned me. Two years after we married, I grew concerned because of her deep melancholia, her sadness. In the beginning her despondency came and went, but as time passed she gradually sank into the very depths of despair.

"I spent every waking hour caring for her." He blinked back a tear. "Finally we had no money left. What was I to do? Then the opportunity came for me to enter the fur business, and I leaped at the chance. For Alfaretta's sake. Even though Dr. Mulgrave held out no hope, I vowed to do everything in my power to keep from sending her to a Canadian Bedlam. Leaving her in the care of a cousin, I journeyed here."

Wolf paused, started to speak, stopped, then began again. "How can you ever forgive me?" he asked. "Since I hadn't tasted freedom in many years, I became intoxicated with it. For a brief wonderful moment I must have imagined myself to be without obligations. So I lied to you and to George Stansbury and everyone else. I misrepresented myself. If only I could have it to do over, I'd alter so much, make so many amends, but we're never granted that wish, are we? What am I to do, Marianne?"

She stared at him, overwhelmed by his tale of suffering, angry with him for deceiving her, yet saddened by the hopelessness of his plight. Surely not even one of Lucinda's heroes had faced such a dilemma.

"There's only one course of action open to you," Marianne told him. "You must return to the woman you vowed to love and honor in sickness and in health. You should do your best to cheer and comfort her for the rest of her life; it's your bounden duty."

"I knew what your answer would be," Wolf said. "There's no other honorable way, and despite appearances, I consider myself to be an honorable man. Though a very human one subject to all the frailties of mankind."

"You should have never yielded to the temptation to pass yourself off as an unmarried man. Never."

As she spoke of temptation, Marianne flushed. She'd been tempted herself and had not resisted. How could she have been so imprudent? Have so misjudged him? If only he had been free, all might be different. There was, however, nothing to be gained by hoping for the never-was, never-to-be. What was done, was done; she must try to go on with her life as best she could, her lesson learned. Trust not in men.

Slowing the matched bays to a walk, Wolf took her hand in his. She started to pull away, but he tightened his grip. *I won't make a spectacle by struggling,* she told herself, all the while denying any pleasure in his touch.

He held her hand while he spoke. "I'll never forget you," he said. "If you ever cared for me, even in the slightest, I want you to promise me something."

She drew in a breath, afraid to look at him for fear tears would spill onto her cheeks.

He pressed her hand. "You must promise you'll forget me and whatever I may have meant to you. You have to put the past behind you, live in the here and now as you prepare to face the future. Will you promise me that, Marianne?"

Blinking to hold back the tears, she nodded. She was afraid to speak, for if she did, she knew she would break into sobs.

"I have a wish for you," Wolf said, "a wish I make with all my heart. Somehow I know it will come true because you're too fine a person to be denied a woman's fulfillment in life. Who he will be, I cannot say. He may be a tradesman like myself; he may be a gentleman of the ton; he may even be a lord. He may not appear for a year or two years or three; he may make his appearance tomorrow. When he does, you'll recognize him, Marianne, and you must not allow any remembrance of me to stand in the way of two people destined to meet and, God willing, find love and happiness with one another."

"I can't put my feelings into words." Marianne smiled through her tears, struck anew by the unselfish nobility of his thoughts. If only she could match his idealism, his ability to think not of himself but of her.

Wolf in the meantime grimaced as he experienced a strong revulsion to what he was doing. He was not deceitful by nature, and his masquerade as Wolfson Clinton, at first a lark, soon went against his grain. His lies had multiplied alarmingly, and his guilt had grown and grown until the burden was well-high insupportable.

He should tell Marianne the truth and have done with lies; he *would* tell her the truth, come what may. Perhaps in time she'd realize he had practiced his deception for her sake, because he loved her. He knew now that love couldn't be built on a foundation of mistrust. By confessing to her he would atone, in part, for his dishonor.

"Marianne," he said urgently, "there's something I must confess to you. Will you promise to hear me out, to refrain from speaking until I have done with it?"

She looked at him in surprise. What more, she wondered, could he possibly tell her? And why did his voice sound so odd? Most unlike the Wolf she was used to. Her natural skepticism came flooding back, her distrust of all men who protested too much. His vacillation caused her to suspect some of his story was at least in part askew, and yet she couldn't put her finger on the source of her nagging disbelief.

His blue eyes peered intently at her; his hand, warm and comforting, still covered hers. Wolf leaned toward her, and for an instant she allowed herself to be mesmerized by his nearness, by his earnestness, by the plea evident in his expression.

To break the spell, she deliberately looked away from him at the passing carriages, at the same time deftly removing her hand from his. "We were just speaking of Rolissa," she said brightly to mask her perturbation, "and there she is."

Wolf followed her gaze to Rolissa, riding in her yellow phaeton behind two spanking chestnuts, a blue parasol above her head, her light brown hair in ringlets tied with a red ribbon. He glanced beyond Rolissa to a raised promenade where a fsahionably dressed gentleman leaned on his cane, his eyes fixed on the phaeton and its occupant.

Wolf gasped. Shocked and dismayed, he didn't now what to think or what to do. His whole scheme stood in danger of unraveling, not by his own confession which would, after all, have a certain drama, perhaps even a touch of panache, but through Marianne's discovery of his masquerade.

The gentleman on the promenade was Wolfson Clinton, the real, the actual Wolfson Clinton, his black beard trimmed, no longer garbed as a rustic but as a gentleman, an almost identical copy of the false Wolf Clinton except for the color of his pantaloons and a red boutonniere.

Good God, what was he to do? he wondered. At any moment Marianne would see the real Clinton and uncover his deception.

Frantically, he searched ahead of him seeking a roadway into which to turn the curricle. There was none. He slowed the horses, made fast the reins, seized Marianne by the shoulders and pulled her to him, kissing her.

She struggled to free herself. Wolf persisted, holding her close, his lips to hers, enjoying the kiss despite his desperation. Looking ahead, he saw they were not yet past the promenade. Still he held

164

her. At last the promenade was behind them. He released her.

He expected her to strike him with her clenched hand. She didn't. Flushed, she stared straight ahead. "Take me home," she told him, her voice quivering with emotion. Anger, he was certain. And who could blame her?

Wolf urged the bays on. He considered telling her the truth, but in her present state, she was certain to be unreasonable. It would be best to hold his tongue. The moment for confession had slipped by him, was lost forever, so he drove without speaking to the Hilton town house. Yet even now he didn't regret the kiss.

Leaping to the pavement, he hurried around the curricle. By the time he reached the other side of the carriage, Marianne was walking up the front steps. He started to follow. Without looking back, she opened the door and, going in, slammed it behind her.

Wolf stared at the closed door for a long minute before slowly returning to the curricle. Swinging the bays around the square, he looked back, and thinking he saw the flutter of a curtain in the town house, he tipped his hat before driving to the Park, to the promenade. Wolf Clinton was no longer there. Though he searched the roadways in all directions, he did not find him. With a sigh he abandoned his search and, bowed in defeat, drove toward the livery.

He shook his head. What was to have been Wolf Clinton's final day on Earth had ended with an unexpected resurrection.

Chapter Twelve

Marianne, drawn from the morning room by the sound of Paul's piano playing, entered the foyer, where the splash of the fountain mingled with the strains of the ballad. She didn't recognize the melody, so she decided it must be one of the songs the boy had composed in the last few days.

The lugubrious song matched her own mood, and not for the first time, she wondered if Paul could, at least occasionally, be as unhappy as she. Usually Paul seemed content. He loved his new-found musical ability, played constantly, and looked forward with eager anticipation to the visits of Madame Thorwald, the piano teacher recommended by Calivari.

At other times, despite her own doting attentions and those of Lucinda, Mrs. Featheringill, and all of the female servants, Paul appeared lost, adrift. At those times she wondered if he missed his old life amidst the soot and ashes of the chimneys. No, that was hardly possible, and yet Paul's moodiness troubled her. A child should be happy.

Marianne looked through the cascading waters of the fountain and saw a man approaching from the entry hall. She caught her breath, her hand flying to her mouth. Wolf Clinton. He had come back. Her heart lurched wildly, sending unexpected joy surging within her.

How foolish you are! Marianne chided herself. *How many times in the last week have you thought you saw Wolf? Five? Six? Seven? Several times while shopping, twice looking down from the library window into the square, on another occasion while riding in the Park. Each time "Wolf Clinton" turned out to be a stranger.*

Not that she wanted to see him again. Nor was it likely she would, for by now he must be hundreds of miles from London sailing westward across the Atlantic on his way home to Canada and his poor, demented wife, Alfaretta. He had deceived her, Marianne told herself, she hated him for it, and that was the end of the matter. If only she could convince her errant heart that Wolf was gone forever.

Her visitor circled the foyer, and as soon as he was no longer partially concealed by the falling waters, she recognized Lord Brandon. Quelling her disappointment, she smiled and walked quickly forward to greet him.

Lord Brandon bowed over her hand. "Marianne, it's so good to see you again. I came here the moment I arrived from Bath."

He looked different, she noted, a shade older, a trifle more pensive, perhaps. Did his clothes,

168

muted grays, bespeak a less flamboyant outlook on life? His expression puzzled her, for though he seemed genuinely glad to see her, Marianne nevertheless detected a wariness in his eyes she had never noticed before.

She put her thoughts into words. "Somehow," she told him, "you look as if you have lived an entire year in the last month. Is Bath such a sobering place?"

"Bath had naught to do with it, though I agree I've changed. For the better, I trust." He smiled. "And you, Marianne, have you changed? In appearance, surely, you're even more beautiful than I remembered."

His tone seemed different as well, serious, almost somber. She scarcely heard his complimentary words as his blue eyes gazed intently into hers, sending a perplexing frisson of delight tingling through her. She looked away, frowning. Never before had Lord Brandon made her feel that way.

"The music you hear is Paul playing the pianoforte," she said to cover her confusion. "The climbing boy who's living here."

"Paul's fame has spread to Bath," he told her.

They walked to the doorway of the sitting room and looked inside. Mrs. Featheringill nodded in the corner while Paul sat on the high piano chair fashioned especially for him, jotting musical notes on a paper on the rack above the keyboard. After a few minutes, he stopped writing and played, the music slow and plaintive.

"Doesn't he play beautifully?" Marianne asked.

"Exceedingly well. Yet his song is so sad." Lord Brandon glanced from Mrs. Featheringill to Marianne. "I wonder if he feels somewhat lost in this house of women."

That could be Paul's problem, she told herself. Why did it take Lord Brandon to point it out? After years of living with boys and men, Paul might very well remember their boisterous camaraderie while forgetting their cruelty.

"He reminds me of someone," Lord Brandon said suddenly. "A vague resemblance, no more. Do you see a likeness?"

Marianne studied Paul's thin face, his sloping shoulders, his fair hair. "Actually, no," she said. "If I were forced to choose someone he resembles, it would be you, Brandon."

Lord Brandon looked at her askance, then smiled. "Perhaps it's the Stansburys," he said. "Georgie or the general."

Marianne considered. "He resembles the general more than he does Georgie, though his hair is as fair as yours." She looked more closely at Lord Brandon's hair. "Although surely yours has darkened since last we met."

"My valet took ill," Lord Brandon explained hurriedly, "and in Bath I was forced to employ a barber who cajoled me into trying a hair cream of his own devising. With the result you see." He shook his head. "But I didn't hasten here to discuss my tonsorial mishaps. I came to invite you to my balloon ascension."

"You're going aloft in a balloon? How exciting!" Her enthusiasm quickly lapsed into suspicion, and a hard look came into her eyes. "Is this another race you and Georgie have conjured up?"

"Not at all, I've forsworn racing. You look dubious, yet it's God's truth. I may have had something of the sort in the back of my mind when I met M. Delacroix, but now the two of us intend to use our ascension to conduct scientific experiments in the upper atmosphere. We've carted the balloon to a barn at Tattersall's to prepare for the flight. It should take place four weeks from today, depending on the weather."

"You *have* changed."

"I trust I have. I want to change, I intend to change, I will change. I only pray the altering of my ways doesn't come too late. I've wiped my slate clean, Marianne. This is a new beginning for me. Be patient with me, since I may, like a schoolboy encountering a subject for the first time, make more than my share of mistakes, may even fall into a filthy puddle or two along the way; yet I mean to do my best."

She regarded him skeptically. "The waters of Bath must have purifying qualities that even Beau Nash never discovered."

"I swear to you the spa at Bath played no part in any decisions of mine. No part at all." Lord Brandon looked down into the fountain's pool at the goldfish darting to and fro, blissfully unconcerned with human strivings and failings. "Do you remember you once quoted Jonathan Swift to me, claiming I was constant only in my inconstancy? No longer is that true, Marianne."

To her surprise, she believed him. This new-born Brandon not only surprised her, but she actually found herself respecting him. There was something else about him, however, that gave her pause, a feeling not so easily defined. An excitement when she was close to him, a quickening of her pulses, an expectancy.

"I intend," Lord Brandon went on, "to follow the good advice of yourself and others and pay more heed to my tenants at Scarborough Hall. Even if doing so forces me to desert London and you from time to time."

"Lord Brandon, you do amaze me." Did she detect a note of mild censure in his voice? Had she, perhaps, been too insistent that he change his ways?

"I'll take my leave, then," Lord Brandon said, "while you're still in a state of amazement. Certainly amazement is better than disinterest or irritation or anger. If I may call upon you again, my own state of mind will be in a state bordering on rapture."

"I'd like to see you again, Lord Brandon."

Her words, Marianne realized, were more than mere politeness. She wanted Lord Brandon to call on her, this new Lord Brandon. Not that she believed he'd be capable of following this more sober regimen forever, but with her encouragement, he might be able to mend his ways for a while.

She walked with him to the street door, standing at the top of the steps with the June sun warm on her face as the Brandon coachman swung down the steps and opened the carriage door. Lord Brandon leaned from the window and, as the carriage pulled away, tipped his hat in a farewell salute.

Marianne drew in a sharp breath. The gesture was only too familiar. Someone else had raised his hat in the same way only a few days before. Who? But of course she knew. The man she wished to forget forever, Wolf Clinton. How was it two men as dissimiliar as Wolf and Lord Brandon gestured in exactly the same manner? Or were they as dissimilar as it appeared on the surface? Turning, she walked slowly into the town house, knitting her brow as a suspicion began to gnaw insidiously at her.

The sun from the windows in the dome high above her head slanted through the falling waters of the fountain in the foyer, creating a rainbow of colors, the luminescent glow shimmering with breathtaking splendor. Suddenly a cloud covered the sun, and the rainbow vanished.

"The rainbow comes and goes, and lovely is the rose." A line from a Wordsworth poem, she recalled. "Constant only in his inconstancy." Those were Swift's words.

Her suspicion blossomed into an awful probability. Lord Brandon hadn't recognized the quote as Swift's when she'd first used it several months before, she was convinced of that, and yet he'd readily identified it today. Had Georgie told him? No, Lord Brandon said he had come directly to the town house on his arrival in London from Bath. He must have learned the source of the quote while taking the waters. Unlikely, yet possible.

When she had seen Lord Brandon through the mist of the fountain, she had mistaken him for Wolf Clinton.

On riding away in his carriage, Lord Brandon had raised his hat, and the gesture reminded her of Wolf Clinton.

Lord Brandon's hair today was much darker than she had ever seen it before. A barber in Bath, he claimed, had done the damage when he put a new concoction to the test. Supposedly, Lord Brandon, who prided himself on his impeccable grooming, had docilely submitted to being the subject of an experiment by an unfamiliar barber. Unlikely, to say the least.

Lord Brandon had changed, had been wary of her, somewhat uncertain of his reception. Why? Because he had started a new life of sobriety and purpose? No, he knew she would applaud his change of direction. Because of her earlier rejection of his suit? Perhaps. Because he had something to conceal, a secret he feared she might discover? Yes, she was all but convinced that was the reason.

The conclusion, though shocking, was inescapable. Wolf Clinton was in reality Lord Brandon in disguise. Wolf Clinton didn't exist except in Brandon's imagination. He'd deceived her. Angered by her rejection, he'd set out to humiliate her before all of London. And would succeed if the truth became known. What a fool she'd been!

Marianne sank onto the low wall surrounding the pool, feeling as weak as if Lord Brandon had

174

actually struck her. Lightheaded, she had difficulty catching her breath. The foyer whirled about her.

Dipping her hand into the pool, she splashed cold water on her face. At long last the whirling lessened and stopped, and her breathing slowed. Could she be mistaken about Lord Brandon's deception? There existed little room for doubt. Yet she must be certain of his deceit, she told herself, absolutely certain. In her mind she knew he had played an undergame, yet she must also convince her susceptible heart.

Who had Lord Brandon taken into his confidence? Georgie Stansbury, for one. Georgie had known all along! How could he have countenanced such a tawdry masquerade? She'd face him down and demand the truth.

Her mind made up, she started toward the sitting room to write a note asking Georgie to call on her without delay. At the doorway, she stopped. Poor Georgie, loyal, innocent, bumbling Georgie. How could she blame him when she knew he'd lay down his life for Lord Brandon? He'd never betray his best friend, not with words, yet if she confronted him with her knowledge, his demeanor was bound to give him away. And ever afterward he'd consider himself a traitor to Lord Brandon.

There must be another way to confirm her suspicions, a way that avoided injuring Georgie.

Old Mrs. Featheringill still sat on the other side

of the sitting room, embroidering red and blue kings and queens along the border of a linen teacloth. She glanced up and smiled when Marianne entered the room, then returned to her needlework.

. Marianne recalled the day Wolf Clinton first visited the Hilton town house, and pictured Mrs. Featheringill staring at him in surprise, Wolf kneeling beside her chair and saying, with emphasis, "I'm Wolf Clinton."

Marianne crossed the room and knelt before her much as Wolf had done. The old woman laid her embroidery hoop on her lap.

"I want to talk to you about Wolfson Clinton," Marianne said. When Mrs. Featheringill nodded encouragingly, she went on. "Mr. Clinton was actually Lord Brandon in disguise, wasn't he?"

"Young gentlemen will play their pranks." Mrs. Featheringill smiled. "My cousin Jarvis was a great prankster. The men were crueler in those days. I recall the time Jarvis borrowed the coffin. I think it was Jarvis. Or was it my cousin Archibald, Beau we always called him, the one who suffered so horribly later on with the gout? Archibald wasn't actually my cousin, of course; he was my mother's cousin, making him my second cousin or is it my great cousin or perhaps my first cousin once removed? Or was it his father who borrowed the coffin? No, his father was Henry, who was lamed by his horse on his wedding day. Henry never suffered from the gout; he was one of the few Sinclair men who didn't. My mother maintained

God was making amends to him for his being lamed by the horse."

"You were telling me about Lord Brandon," Marianne reminded her.

"I'm coming to that. Jarvis, it *was* Jarvis, not Archibald. He borrowed a coffin, placed his footman inside to masquerade as the corpse, set the coffin upright in front of old Kramer's house, and knocked. Kramer's maid fainted dead away when she opened the door. Cousin Jarvis told the story for years afterward. A great prankster, Jarvis was." Mrs. Featheringill frowned. "Or was it Archibald after all?"

Marianne realized that Mrs. Featheringill hadn't told her in so many words whether Wolfson Clinton was, in fact, Lord Brandon in disguise.

"You thought Lord Brandon was playing a prank?" she asked.

"What other reason could he have had, appearing here with his hair blackened and wearing that awful beard? Don't tell me you didn't recognize him?"

"Not at first," Marianne admitted.

Mrs. Featheringill had managed to surprise her just as she had many times in the past. The old woman seemed to doze her days away, and yet she had immediately penetrated Lord Brandon's disguise.

"He had the Brandon walk," Mrs. Featheringill explained, "even though he limped a bit. His grandfather had it, as did his father. I suppose I should have spoken out, but I took it for granted

177

that you were party to the prank."

If only you had told me, Marianne thought, *if only I'd known from the beginning. Yet how could I have been taken in by Lord Brandon's deception when the truth was instantly clear to Mrs. Featheringill? Did I want to be deceived? What an odd idea, of course I didn't; no one wants to be fooled. I can't let Mrs. Featheringill see my distress, though; the infirmities of old age are enough of a burden for her without adding my troubles to them.*

"No great harm's been done," she assured the older woman. "The prank's at an end; Lord Brandon had discarded his beard and become himself once more."

"I'm glad. I've always liked the boy; I hope you won't be too harsh with him." Mrs. Featheringill closed her eyes and smiled in reminiscence. "I remember his grandfather well. John. No, John was his father; his grandfather's name was Clarence. Or was it the other way round? Yes, his grandfather was John. A charming, top-of-the-trees lad, he quite swept all of us off our feet. A wonderful dancer. He was well on his way to becoming a rake, however, when his mother arranged a marriage to settle him down. Most amazing happenstance, he fell in love with the girl and *did* settle down." Mrs. Featheringill opened her eyes and looked at Marianne with a surprisingly shrewd gaze. "Things don't usually come out the way we plan, do they?"

"No, not at all."

"And that's probably for the best. Nothing

makes a person unhappier than getting precisely what she wants. The pleasures of life are in the seeking, I've always maintained.'' Again Mrs. Featheringill closed her eyes, this time leaning back in her chair. After a few minutes her breathing became regular, and Marianne saw that the old woman had fallen asleep.

As Marianne stood, the realization of what had happened returned, not with an overwhelming rush, but as an unremitting throb of pain. Brandon had betrayed and humiliated her. All his protestations of affection, whether as Wolf or as himself, were worthless. Tears scalded her eyes; a sob caught in her throat.

She left the sitting room and ran up the stairs, blindly seeking her bedroom, changed her mind on reaching the hallway, opened the door to the attic, and closed it behind her, breathing in the mustiness of this unusued portion of the upper-most floor.

At the top of the attic stairs, she looked around her, blinking back tears. Two oval windows overlooked the square. The slope of the roof created dark recesses under the eaves, and down one side of the room brick chimneys rose one after the other from the floor to the roof.

Her first inclination had been to flee to her bedroom, hurl herself on her bed and cry until no tears remained unshed. Instead, instinct had brought her here where she felt safe and protected by her memories of the past. The light from the two windows was dim, and she hadn't brought a lamp; but by peering into the gloom, she was able to make out the bulk of an old, black brass-bound trunk near one of the chimneys.

Dropping to her knees in front of the trunk, she lifted the lid and looked inside. Yellowed newspapers lay piled at one end, dresses she had worn as a child had been neatly folded beside the papers, and two forgotten dolls and a child's jewelbox rested next to the dresses. Opening the box, she found a necklace of shells, a gilded clasp, a ring with a large red stone, and several silver buttons. She tried to slide the ring onto her little finger, but it wouldn't fit; so she returned it to the box.

About to close the jewelbox, Marianne remembered its secret compartment and drew in her breath. Her fingers trembled as she slid aside the latch to release the tiny hidden drawer. When it popped open, she stared at its contents for a long moment before touching the pointed piece of flint with a hesitant forefinger, her heart thudding in her chest.

"What's that there?"

Paul's voice startled her, and she whirled around.

"I didn't know you were in the attic," she said.

"I likes it up here." He pointed to the open drawer. "That be some kinda special stone?" he asked.

Marianne swallowed her instinctive impulse to push the compartment closed and return the jewelbox to the trunk. This was hers; this was private. But Paul, who hardly ever spoke, had finally shown interest in something besides music.

"This is an Indian arrowhead," she said, surprised that she sounded so calm. "Hold out your hand." Lifting the flint shard from the drawer, she placed it on his palm. "Across the ocean in America, the red savages use these stones as points for their arrows."

Paul's eyes widened as he glanced from her to the sharp flint. He felt the point with his finger.

"My father gave the arrowhead to me when I wasn't much older than you," she went on. "We were going to sail to America. . . ." Her voice trailed off, and she stared blindly past him.

Hesitantly, Paul touched her arm. His tentative gesture of comfort brought tears to her eyes. "I want you to keep the arrowhead," she told him, trying to smile. "It will be your good luck charm."

His eyes lit up. "Ain't never had a lucky piece before," he said.

"You do now."

Paul's fist closed around the arrowhead, and he threw his arms around her neck and hugged her. A moment later he was clattering down the attic stairs, whistling.

Marianne looked after him, brushing the tears from her eyes. It was the first time Paul had shown any affection toward her, and she treasured the moment. *No matter what happens to me,* she vowed, *he* will *have good fortune.*

Finding her father's gift had evoked the magic as well as the grief of the past. But she was an adult; she knew better than to be taken in by make-believe. Shouldn't she also be able to dispose of long-ago disappointments? Just as she'd given away the arrowhead?

She closed the jewelbox, returned it to the trunk, shut the lid and sat on top of it. Her fingers idly roved over the metal studs and fastenings. The trunk, she knew, had been her mother's and had accompanied her to Venice, to Naples, to Rome, to Paris. Wouldn't it be wonderful to pack up and leave London, to spend the summer on the boulevards of the French capital, on the beaches along the Normandy coast, or exploring the valley of the Rhone?

She shook her head. She was not about to turn her back when faced with adversity, to run and hide. She wouldn't attempt to recreate a dead past or flee to exotic climes when beset by troubles.

How passive she'd been these last few months! Ever since Lord Brandon had asked for her hand, she'd allowed him to lead her as though she had a ring through her nose, to pull her this way and then shove her that way as if she were as docile and mindless as the dolls in the trunk. The time had come for her to take her future into her own hands.

If only she were a man. There was no doubt in her mind that men had all the better of it; if she were a man there'd be no question what she would do. She pictured herself striding into White's, and imagined Lord Brandon rising from the depths of his armchair, a glass of port in his hand.

"Lord Brandon," she'd say, "I demand an apology for your base and despicable behavior."

Lord Brandon would try to laugh the affair away. "An apology for a jape? For a masquerade meant only in sport? You must know I never intended you harm."

When Marianne didn't answer, the insincere smile faded from Brandon's lips, and one corner of his mouth twitched. He placed his glass on the table beside him.

"Do you apologize, sir," she demanded, "or do you not?"

Lord Brandon drew himself up to his full height. "Never," he said.

Grasping her gloves in one hand, she struck him across the face. The clubroom suddenly hushed. All eyes were on them. Lord Brandon flushed in anger.

"Name your seconds," he told her. . . .

Dawn. The carriages silhouetted against the pale light of early morning. Streamers of mist rising from the river. The surgeon standing to one side holding his small black bag. Lord Brandon firing first, missing. She taking careful aim, firing. Lord Brandon clutching his shoulder—she had purposely aimed so high so as not to kill him— reluctantly nodding, acknowledging her superior markswomanship.

Marianne opened her eyes, the vision vanished, and her momentary smile of triumph left her lips. Daydreaming would get her nowhere; she wasn't about to fight a duel with Lord Brandon.

Nor did she intend to accept the humiliation he

sought to bring down on her. There were ways other than dueling to seek retribution. There must be. And she did have a small advantage. She knew Lord Brandon had deceived her, yet neither he nor anyone other than Mrs. Featheringill was aware of her knowledge. She would tell no one and swear Mrs. Featheringill to silence.

She would *not* confront Lord Brandon. Instead, she'd play a waiting game to lull him into complacency and carelessness. And when the time came, when she spied her opportunity, she'd be ready. She didn't know what that opportunity might be or in what form it would arrive, but she'd recognize it when the time came. She smiled with the bitter foretaste of her revenge.

Marianne rose from the trunk, walked down the attic stairs and closed the door firmly behind her. There were more ways than one to right the wrong he'd done her; as a woman she possessed more deadly weapons than pistols.

Chapter Thirteen

After Lord Brandon and George left the Kravitz Fur Warehouse by the side door, they stood undecided on the dirt footpath watching laden drays rumble past them on their way from the nearby Thames' docks. On the other side of the cobbled street, hod carriers climbed long plank ramps to the tops of the partly finished walls of a textile factory.

"Good to get out-of-doors," George said, "where the only foul smell is the London smoke."

Lord Brandon glanced sideways at him, wondering if his friend was being facetious. No, he decided, Georgie seldom attempted dry witticisms; he said exactly what came into his mind.

"I find the smoke of London as disheartening as our search," Lord Brandon said. "Mr. Wolfson Clinton seems to have disappeared into thin air."

"Dash it all, Brandon, look on the bright side. The man's undoubtedly on his way to America and his wife just as you told Marianne. The reason we can't locate the chap is he's decamped bag and baggage."

"Georgie, at times I find your unflagging optimism damned depressing."

"Sorry, Brandon. The way God made me, I'm afraid. Too late to change my stripes now." George tapped the crown of his natty gray top hat to set it more firmly on his head. "Even if I wanted to. Which I do not."

"Lately, Georgie, I've detected a new spirit in you. You're more independent. Not that I object, being self-sufficient becomes a man."

"Lucinda's doing," George said proudly. "Claims I should stand up for myself. Not always agree with you and Chichester and the others, the general included. Difficult to do, you know, because usually I do agree." He paused. "Damned fine girl, Lucy."

"Women are never satisfied until they reshape men into their notion of the ideal."

"Not Lucy. She never insists. She suggests. Wants to help. Makes a man feel top-of-the-trees, having a friend who takes such an interest in him."

"So you consider Lucinda only a friend?" Lord Brandon's voice rose in surprise.

"Lucy and I are the best of friends. Get along splendidly. Don't rock the boat, I say, when the sea's calm and the sailing's smooth."

"I have a rather closer tie in mind between myself and Marianne," Lord Brandon said. "Which is why we must find Wolf Clinton if he's

186

still in London. And some sixth sense of mine tells me he is here. If Marianne ever met Mr. Clinton and discovered he's been in Paris for the last month, I fear she'd unmask me in an instant. And that would be the end of all my hopes, since she'd never speak to me again. My God, how did I ever get into this imbroglio?''

"Isn't that a Turkish harem?"

"I only wish it were. However, it happens to be a very filthy puddle.''

"Perhaps you fell into the puddle by being too clever by half.''

Lord Brandon gave George a hard look, then shrugged and smiled. "Whatever got me into this coil, it's now up to me to pull myself out. And to do that we must find Wolf Clinton. Our best plan is to separate so we each follow a different avenue of attack. I'll question the remaining fur merchants and inquire at the hotels. You, Georgie, inquire of everyone who knows Wolf—myself in the role of Wolf, that is—to discover whether they've seen him in the last week. And where they saw him.''

"Glad to help, Brandon. I'll pay calls on Harriet Ramsden and Lucy and Marianne. What excuse will I use for wanting to find Wolf Clinton?''

"Tell them he owes you more than a little blunt. A gambling debt, perhaps. They'll readily believe that.''

"No truth to the tale, though. By God, Brandon, I don't want to lie. Especially not to my friends.''

"This is all in a good cause, Georgie. But if you

balk at a fib or two, hint at your reason for wanting to find him. A mere suggestion's enough to set most women to suspecting the worst of a man."

"A hint or two. The very thing, Brandon."

"And inquire of your father."

"We're rather at loggerheads, Father and I," George said. "As usual. I try to follow Lucy's advice and stand up to the general. Easier said than done. I'll ask him about Wolf, though."

"Don't forget Rolissa Highsmith. I have to put modesty aside and admit she was quite taken with me in my role of Wolf Clinton when we met at the musicale. And when I spied the real Wolf in the Park, he seemed more than a little enraptured by the sight of Miss Highsmith riding by. So you must speak to Rolissa."

"I'd rather you talked to her, Brandon."

"Oh? Most men would leap at the chance for an intimate tête-à-tête with Rolissa."

George shifted from one foot to the other, pulling his gloves snug on his fingers one by one. "To tell the truth," he admitted, "I find her rather off-putting."

"I don't follow you. Rolissa's been called many things, but off-putting?"

"Dash it all, Brandon, I'm afraid of the girl," George blurted. "There you have it. Can't help being afraid. Just am."

"Rolissa's actually quite harmless. I even suspect her coquettishness is only a ploy and not for the usual reason." Lord Brandon put his hand on his friend's arm. "Hasn't Lucy said you should stand up for yourself? This is a chance of a lifetime. She'd want you to call on Rolissa to help you overcome your trepidation. Think of it this way, you'll be seeing Rolissa for Lucy's sake."

"Hadn't seen it in that light before." George stood tall and threw back his shoulders. "I'll ask Rolissa about Wolf Clinton. For Lucy's sake."

"That's a good chap. I suggest you pay your call on Miss Highsmith before you talk to the others. So you won't have time to waver in your resolve."

"You're right, Brandon, as always. Leave me at Jason's livery and I'll start my rounds with a visit to the Highsmiths. If Wolf Clinton is still in London, between the two of us we'll find him before the dawn of another day."

"For my sake," Lord Brandon said, "we'd better."

"Georgie," Rolissa suggested, "why don't we steal away into the rose garden?"

Taking his hand, she led him from the house into the garden at the rear of the Kier-Windom mansion and onto a pebbled path that meandered among the red and white blooms of the roses. The scent, intoxicating to George at first, quickly became overpowering.

As soon as he politely could, George disengaged his hand from Rolissa's, ostensibly to adjust his indigo cravat.

She smiled up at him in her winsome way. "We'll sit in the arbor," she said. Lowering her voice to a conspiratorial whisper, she added, "Where Mother won't be able to watch our every move from her window."

Good God, George thought, *what have I let myself in for?* Refusing to panic, he looked from the corner of his eye at Rolissa, her brown hair teased into uncountable ringlets, her dress a deep yellow in a cloth he recognized as Italian crape. The neckline he found remarkably unsettling, not because it was square, but because it was low enough to reveal the provocative swell of her bosom.

"Do you like it?" she asked.

George reddened guiltily. "Wh-what?" he stammered.

"My new afternoon dress, of course."

He started to look once more at the dress, then immediately glanced away, knowing he wouldn't be able to keep his gaze from the enticing curves the dress only partially concealed. "Ch-charming," he managed to say.

Rolissa's laughter threatened to escalate into a crescendo of giggles. "I don't think we've ever had a good chat," she said when she was again able to speak. "Did you ever consider, Georgie, how very fortunate you are?"

"As a matter of fact, I have." He sighed with relief to have found an innocuous subject.

"Here you are," Rolissa said, "more than content with being the English gentleman you were born to be. If only all of us could be so fortunate. You're inclined to exhibit a touch of naivete, it's true, but most women, myself included, find that trait rather endearing."

George shifted his shoulders uneasily. Why must Rolissa constantly bring the conversation around to men *and* women? He'd much prefer to discuss the sexes one at a time. "I came to ask—" he began.

"First I have a favor to request from you." Rolissa leaned toward him so that her hair lightly brushed his shoulder. "Shall we sit here?"

They had come to an arbor embowered with climbing red roses. Rolissa sat on one side of a wooden bench screened from the house by the proliferation of blooms and patted the other side in invitation. George settled himself as far from her as he thought politeness permitted.

"I desire your opinion, Georgie, as a gentleman of the ton," she told him. Reaching into a pocket of her dress, she brought forth two small vials and held them toward him, one in each hand. "These fragrances were imported from Paris," she explained. "I need your help in choosing the one I should wear on the night of the Midsummer Ball. Will you help me decide, Georgie?"

He had no choice but to nod.

Rolissa placed the vials side by side on the bench and carefully removed their glass stoppers. "I thought I might put some of one scent behind my left ear and some of the other behind my right." She held the stoppers head high. "Or perhaps one on my right cheek and the other on my left so that you could inhale the scents one at a time and

191

choose. But I have a better notion." She held the stoppers next to her creamy skin just above the top of the bodice of her dress.

George drew in his breath in alarm even as he stared at Rolissa in fascinated anticipation.

"Hold out your hands, Georgie," she instructed him. "Don't be shy; they'll cause you no harm."

When he held his hands toward her, palms up, she deftly rubbed the stopper of one vial across his left wrist, the other across his right. When he didn't move, she said, "Raise them to your nose one by one, Georgie, and then give me your considered opinion which you prefer."

He did as she told him. One wrist gave off the scent of roses, the other of lilies of the valley.

George smelled his wrists again and then pursed his lips, considering. "I prefer the lilies of the valley," he said finally. "Reminds me of my grandmother. Because of her garden. My grandmother on my father's side."

"Thank you, Georgie." Rolissa smiled up at him. "From now on, every time I breathe in the scent of lilies of the valley, I'll think of you. And of your grandmother as well." She squeezed his hand. "Now that you've helped me, I'll try my utmost to do the same for you."

"I'm searching for Mr. Wolfson Clinton. Not important. A little matter between gentlemen."

"Wolf Clinton!" Rolissa's vehemence surprised George. "I met him at the musical evening at the Hiltons'," she said, quickly regaining her composure. "Then I saw him some days later in the

Park, and he stared right through me as if he'd never seen me before in his life." She raised her eyes to his. "You don't consider me so instantly forgettable, do you, Georgie?"

He shook his head vigorously. What could he tell her? That one Wolf Clinton had been Lord Brandon in disguise and the other the genuine Canadian fur trader? Hardly.

"I trust not," Rolissa said. "In the last few days, I've not seen the man again even though I've driven in the Park at precisely the same time and I'm certain I would have noticed him if he'd been there. With his black beard and all. I don't know what to make of him nor do I know what's become of the man. If you do find him, Georgie, you may tell him I consider him to be excessively rude and that I said I never wanted to set eyes on him again."

"I can understand why you wouldn't want to see him again. After the way he behaved."

"Georgie," Rolissa said, "I didn't say I didn't want to see him; I said to tell him I didn't want to see him."

"Dash it all, Rolissa, what's the difference?"

"When you understand that, Georgie, perhaps you'll begin to understand women."

George found Lucinda sitting at the writing table in the Hilton library, her hands clasped in front of her, a frown on her face.

"I'll never write another word for the rest of my life," she told him, "not if I live to be a hundred.

My muse has deserted me, fled never to return. I'm not an author; my father always told me I wasn't, yet I refused to believe him. I thought my modest little stories were amusing and even at times exciting, but I was wrong. Just as I've been wrong about so many other things lately.''

"*I* enjoy your stories, Lucy.''

"You don't really mean it; you say that to try to make me feel better, Georgie.'' She shook her head. ''I'm sorry, I can't think of you as George, you're Georgie, and I'll have to call you Georgie.''

"Perfectly all right, Lucy. Everybody does.''

"No one really likes or appreciates my writing, scribbling you all call it; and you come here, Georgie, after I haven't seen you in heaven knows how long and say *you* like it, and you expect me to believe you.''

"It's the God's truth, Lucy. Have you forgotten I was here to see you the day before yesterday? Been frightfully busy since then searching for Wolf Clinton. He's why I'm here now. Want to ask if you've seen him. Not the only reason I came, don't think it is.''

"Of course I haven't seen Mr. Clinton; he's sailing back to Canada to be with his poor wife. I only wish I could sail away across the seven seas to Australia, to parts unknown, to terra incognita. No one would know I was gone if I did.'' Tears rolled down her cheeks.

George knelt beside her and took her hand in his. "I'd miss you, Lucy,'' he said. "Something dreadful.''

She drew in a sobbing breath. "Georgie!" she cried. "What is that scent?" She breathed deeply. "I can't decide whether you reek of roses or lilies of the valley."

"A bit of both, actually." When she looked at him in a speaking way, he explained, "Rose scent on my right wrist, lily of the valley on my left."

"I just happen to know who favors those particular scents. Rolissa Highsmith."

George stood and retreated a few steps. From the frying pan into the fire. Flustered, he could think of nothing to say in his defense.

"You admit it, then," she said. "You've been with Rolissa, of all people."

"Only saw her to ask her a-a-about Wolf," George stammered. All at once he had an inspiration. "Actually, I saw her because of you, Lucy."

"Because of me." Each word was a sharp sliver of ice. "How, pray tell, did I have anything to do with your hobnobbing or whatever else you might have been doing with Rolissa?"

"You told me to be more forthright. Be less timid where women are concerned. So I went to see Rolissa. Good place to start, I thought."

"I see, George. I understand perfectly." She dabbed at her eyes. "You spent your afternoon making love to Rolissa Highsmith to please me. Because I told you to. At least that's your excuse. After weeks of unexplained absence, you come to see me, saturated with Rolissa's scents. George, please leave. Please leave at once."

"But Lucy. Let me explain. Wasn't that way in

the slightest. Perfectly harmless conversation with Rolissa. She only wanted me to choose a scent for her."

"Rolissa has clearly led you down the garden path."

"She did, as a matter of fact. How in the world did you ever know?"

"You see, I was right." Her words sprang at him as a cat might spring at a mouse.

"Not the way you think. A real garden, a real path. Please don't cry, Lucy, it hurts me to see you cry. Can't abide it at all."

She turned her head away. "Leave me now, George. I'm certain Rolissa Highsmith will be most happy to comfort you if you feel any distress, which I very much doubt you do. All you'll have to do is wait your turn."

George started to speak, shook his head, turned and fled from the room. He hesitated just outside the door, debating whether to go back to plead his case. No, there was no talking to Lucy when she was in this mood; better leave her alone for a while.

Gradually he became aware of an eerie silence in the foyer. After a moment's thought, he realized the fountain wasn't working. Surprised, he slowly circled the foyer, meeting Marianne in the entrance hall. Judging by the parcels she and her maid carried, she had just returned from shopping.

"Is Lucinda feeling better?" Marianne wanted to know.

"Better? She's quite overset. Never going to

write again. Been crying. Accused me of making love to Rolissa Highsmith. Nonsense, of course."

"Oh, dear, I'll go to her. Pay no heed to anything she may have said today, Georgie. Trotter and Sons, you know, decided not to publish her Ramsden novel."

"She never told me. I merely asked after Wolf Clinton, and she flew at me."

"Wolf Clinton? You're looking for Wolf Clinton?" She stared at him in astonishment. When he nodded, she said, "That must mean—" She stopped short.

"Brandon and I are turning London upside down searching for him. A matter between gentlemen."

She frowned. After a moment she started to walk away but stopped and turned to face George. "Georgie Stansbury," she said, "you should be ashamed of yourself."

"Dash it all, Marianne, what did I—?" He broke off, for Marianne had left the hall without a backward glance.

Sighing, George opened the front door. Again he wondered whether he should go to Lucy. No, better wait, he'd only upset her more. Damn Rolissa. He wiped his wrists vigorously on his trousers. Night soil, perfume, one caused as much trouble as the other.

Paul was sitting on the top of the porch steps staring across the square. George rumpled the boy's hair, saying, "Doesn't make sense, Paul, does it now?"

Startled, Paul looked up at him, sprang to his feet and scuttled into the house. George stared after him. "Little boys usually like me," he protested plaintively to anyone who might care to listen.

No one did.

Returning to London after his visit to Harriet Ramsden at Litchfield Hall, George arrived at his father's house shortly after ten in the evening. The general, Stimson informed him, was in his study. The "War Room," George called it.

The day had gone badly, George acknowledged to himself as he walked along the red-carpeted hall. He had always believed there was a measurable amount of bad fortune alloted to each person during the course of a year. On this day he was certain he had received all or almost all of his annual quota. Why not, he asked himself, confront the general about Paul and risk receiving the remainder? Have it done with once and for all. Then for the rest of the year he could greet each new day with his customary cheerfulness.

When George knocked and entered the study, the general looked up from a map of the battle fought near Saratoga during the rebellion of the American colonies. Other battle maps were framed on the walls where they shared space with captured regimental flags, medieval weaponry, and paintings of red-coated huntsmen riding to hounds.

"I come from Litchfield Hall." George sat in a dark leather chair across the desk from his father.

The general shoved his map to one side. "And how is Miss Harriet?" he asked.

"I fear I gave you poor advice," George admitted. "About not storming the Hall and making off with the fair damsel."

"Not the first instance of bad advice from you, George. Nor in all likelihood will it be the last. Did she enjoy my flowers?"

"Didn't mention flowers. Said something or other about the latest of your societies."

"Do you mean The City of London Truss Society for the Relief of the Ruptured Poor Throughout the Kingdom?"

"That's the one." George hesitated. "She seemed impatient with the slowness of your campaign. Personal one, not the truss one. Didn't say that in so many words, of course. My impression. For what it's worth."

The general shook his head as though to say, *I fear it's worth damned little.*

"I'm on the lookout for Wolf Clinton," George said. "Harriet hasn't laid eyes on him of late. Thought you might have."

"Not since the night young Paul astounded us with his piano playing."

This was the time, George told himself, to risk severing the thread holding the sword Lord Brandon had positioned over his head. The general had broached the subject of Paul; he hadn't. He'd plunge in, just as Lucy always urged him to do.

"The lad's a prodigy at the pianoforte," George said.

"Agreed."

"There are those who suggest—" George stopped and then started anew. "Some claim to see a resemblance. Between Paul and me."

"Never considered it. No, I can't say I see one."

"And between you and Paul."

"Farfetched." When George didn't go on, the general thrummed his fingers on the desk. "George," he said, "I've been having the devil of a time deciphering what General Burgoyne had in mind at Saratoga. Don't make me work at understanding your cryptic observations as well. If you have aught to say, speak up."

George colored. "I wonder if there might be— Dash it all, is Paul related by blood? To me? To you?"

The general stared at his son. "Are you asking if the lad's a by-blow of mine? Is that it?" His voice was calm. Deadly calm, George thought.

"Yes, sir, it is."

The general pursed his lips. He rose, walked slowly to the cold hearth, put one hand behind his back, turned and walked to stand beside his desk. "Your question, sir," he said, "is impertinent."

George swallowed. "Yes, sir," he said.

"Nevertheless, I'll answer you." He looked over George's head into the darker recesses of his study. "There was a lady," he said, "who shall be nameless, a Viennese, an accomplished pianist. I knew her for one year, eight months, and—" He paused. "And a number of days. There was a child, yes, there was a child."

"Then you *are* Paul's father."

The general hit the desk with his fist. "Hear me out before you speak. The child was a girl." When he went on, the general had filtered all emotion from his voice. "She died two weeks following her birth. Soon afterward the lady in question returned to Austria. She married within the year. Does that answer your question, sir? Are you satisfied?"

"It does, and I am. Sorry, Father, I had to ask."

"And why did you have to? Have you become a gossip, listening to and believing every tale told at Almacks? Do you spend your days at Tatts regaling your cronies with rumors? Do you dine out on Stansbury family skeletons? Have you settled on tale-bearing as your occupation?"

"No, I haven't."

"Take a good hard look at yourself, George. Do you like what you see? Do you even know what you are or what, in a few years, you'll become?"

George rose and faced his father from across the desk. "Only lately have I caught a glimmering of what I am."

"Pray tell me more of this glimmering. I'm waiting, George. I in all honesty want to know."

"I recognized myself in one of Miss Lucy's tales. The hero was a soldier, a captain. The kind of man you always wanted me to be. He led a daring cavalry charge against the French. I knew at once I wasn't that man, never could be, never will be."

"The two of us know all the things you're not. Pray tell me what you are."

"There was another character in the book, the captain's friend. That's what I am, Father, a friend. I help. I support. I comfort. I might even counsel. I'm at hand when I'm needed. I applaud, cheer others on. Give a word of encouragement. Of praise. Of caution where need be. I realize it's not an important calling, being a loyal friend. It can't compare to other occupations such as the killing of American rebels at Saratoga or the slaying of Frenchmen at Waterloo. In a small way, perhaps, and only perhaps, I make someone happier than he was before he met me, give him a boost, give him someone to talk to, send him off with a smile on his face instead of a scowl." George leaned across the desk and met his father's gaze. "That's what I am, Father, and that's what I'll go on being," he said. "And if you don't like it, why, you can go to hell."

George swung on his heel, strode to the door and flung it open.

"George!" The general's voice was a command.

George turned and watched his father walk around from behind his desk.

"George." His father spoke the name more softly. "Will you grant me a favor, George?" he asked.

"What is it?"

Never before had George seen his father so at a

loss for words. At last the general spoke. "Will you be *my* friend, George?" he asked.

George felt a lump rise in his throat. He took a step toward his father, then another. The older man strode to him, his eyes glistening, and took him in his arms. "George," he said. "My son. Georgie, my son."

When, some time later, George left his father's house, a bearded gentleman awaited from on the sidewalk. George stared at him in disbelief. It was Wolf Clinton.

"George Stansbury?" Wolf asked.

George nodded.

"Have you been in hiding?" Wolf demanded. "These last two days I've been searching from one end of London to the other looking for you."

Chapter Fourteen

"What the devil!" George said to Wolf Clinton. "And *I've* been searching for *you*."

"I find that unlikely."

George felt a twinge of annoyance. Why would this man doubt his word? "True nonetheless," he said firmly.

"I would have thought," Wolf said, "that you'd be doing your best to avoid me. A less peaceable man than myself might have been tempted to come looking for you with a pistol in his hand rather than a walking stick."

"Gentlemen don't walk the streets brandishing firearms," George assured him.

"Where I come from they do. Now tell me, Stansbury, who is he?"

"Only too glad to help. If I knew what you wanted."

"As soon as I set foot back in London," Wolf said, "a Mr. Charles Robinson greeted me outside my rooms as a long-lost friend. Knew me from

Tattersall's, he claimed. Wouldn't believe me when I told him I'd never set foot in the place. Then he wanted to know how my good friend George Stansbury was. Later I heard the same rigmarole from others. Pray tell me, Stansbury, who's been impersonating me? And to what end? Money's at the root of this scheme somewhere; I'll stake my bottom dollar on it."

"Don't do it, you'd lose. 'Twasn't money. The reason for the masquerade was a matter of the heart. Of love."

"Love? Are you daft, man?"

"Not at all. It was done for love and only for love. Come along with me, sir, I'd like you to meet John Cornwall, Fifth Earl of Brandon. You'll find him quite overcome by love. . . ."

Lord Brandon, seated in the room of his town house recently refurbished as an office, rose to greet them. Ledgers, account books and assorted invoices lay scattered across the table in front of him.

"Good work, Georgie." Lord Brandon clapped his friend on the shoulder. "You've succeeded where I failed; you've found Mr. Wolfson Clinton."

"Not quite the way of it, Brandon. He found me at my father's house, actually."

Lord Brandon raised his eyebrows before bowing to Wolf. "The result's the same," he said.

The Canadian, glowering first at one and then the other, ignored the bow. "Haven't I met you two before?" he asked.

"You possess a good memory," Lord Brandon told him. "We met a month or more ago at Tart's Turn, a mile or so this side of Litchfield Hall."

"Ah, yes, the Ramsden place." For a moment Wolf seemed lost in contemplation; then he shook his head impatiently as though to banish all distractions. "Your friend, Stansbury here," he said, "admits you impersonated me after I left for Paris. I insist on knowing why."

Lord Brandon closed a ledger and methodically stacked his books and papers on one side of the table. "Either my estate manager is unusually careless," he said to George, "or else he's dishonest. I suspect he's some of both." He sighed. "On all other counts he's the best manager I've ever had. That's the rub to becoming assiduous about your business interests; you resolve one dilemma only to create two or three more." Finally he looked at Wolf. "As for my harmless masquerade," he said, "I did it for love."

"You see," George said triumphantly to Wolf. "My exact words," he told Lord Brandon.

"And, pray tell," Wolf asked, "what did love have to do with it?"

"If you'll but sit down and share a bottle with us," Lord Brandon said, "I'll be most happy to tell you."

With decided ill grace, Wolf sat and accepted a glass of Madeira. As they sipped the wine, Lord Brandon gave a quick sketch of his impersonation of the Canadian, related his intent to impel Marianne into his own arms, and described the unexpected and quite disastrous consequences.

"Serves you damn well right," Wolf said when Lord Brandon finished. He seemed, though, somewhat mollified by the explanation. "You had no cause to steal another man's good name."

"Hoist by his own petard," George put in, "or so my father would say."

"Deserved or no, I've landed in a particularly filthy puddle," Lord Brandon said. "As you can see, Mr. Clinton, your continued presence in London puts my scheme at risk of exposure."

"That's hardly a concern of mine."

"Perhaps not," Lord Brandon agreed. "On the other hand, I may be able to offer you an inducement to speed your departure from London."

"An inducement? Speak plain English, man. You mean a bribe, I take it." Wolf shook his head. "I neither want nor need your money. I went into the fur trade for but one reason, to set aside a certain sum. A large and unexpected order from a group of Parisians permitted me to reach my goal, so I intend to leave the trade within the fortnight. To attend a university."

"You speak like an educated man, so I'm not surprised," Lord Brandon said. "Yet when I saw you disembarking from that Canadian sailing ship, I could have sworn you were an illiterate rustic."

"I thought a rough-hewn appearance would help me sell furs in your country. I was mistaken. London merchants would prefer to deal with a gentleman who knows nothing of furs rather than with a backwoodsman who knows all there is to know."

"Shakespeare and all that?" George asked.

"I beg your pardon, sir."

"At the university. Will you study the classics, Greeks and Romans and Shakespeare and—and the others?"

"No, higher mathematics is my field of study. I graduated three years ago from Dartmouth College in the State of New Hampshire, and now I'm considering taking an advanced degree at Cambridge, the University of Berlin, or the Polytechnic school in Paris."

"You speak German and French?" Lord Brandon asked.

"French fluently, enough German to be understood."

"I imagine," Lord Brandon said, "you must have spent winters snowed in at a mountain cabin with nothing better to do than study languages."

"How on earth did you know?"

"Only hazarding a guess," Lord Brandon admitted.

"Of what use," George asked, "is the study of higher mathematics? No offense meant. Rather curious, you know."

"Men study mathematics," Lord Brandon told him, "so they can become qualified to instruct other young men who in turn instruct still other young men. It's a form of academic perpetual motion."

"There's a smidgen of truth in what you say,"

Wolf said, "but no more than that. One use of mathematics that might interest you, sir," he said to George, "is determining the odds in games of chance. Games such as hazard."

George nodded. "Never thought of that. Might be more to mathematics than meets the eye."

"If you attended the University of Berlin," Lord Brandon mused, "or even the Polytechnic, it would solve my problem. There's no need for you to travel all the way to Canada."

"I have no desire to accommodate you, sir," Wolf told him. "Your playacting may have been as innocent and harmless as you claim, and then again it may not have been."

"Since you're a trader," Lord Brandon suggested, "perhaps we could barter value for value. Are you willing to listen to a proposition?"

"I've told you I have no use for your money."

"It wasn't money I had in mind. Rather, I was thinking of offering to do you a service. It so happens that both Georgie and myself have the honor and the pleasure of being well acquainted with a certain Miss Rolissa Highsmith."

Wolf startled them by springing to his feet and pacing back and forth across the small room. "She's a wonder, isn't she?" he asked. "She's the only woman I've ever seen who could induce a man to give up everything, his fortune, his good name, his prospects, everything he has in the world. I'd be willing to commit murder to have Rolissa. And you say you know her? You'd be willing to introduce me to her?"

"I believe a mutually satisfactory arrangement

might be arrived at," Lord Brandon said. "We have something to offer you, an introduction to the most desirable woman in all of London, while you have the power to grant my wish to avoid Marianne Hilton for as long as you're in England. What do you say, Clinton, can we strike a bargain?"

"We can and we have; I give you my word on it." Wolf eagerly shook hands with both of them. "Tomorrow. You must take me to Rolissa tomorrow morning."

"Hardly the thing," George said. "Has to be the afternoon. Who's up and about before noon?"

"More people than you realize, sir," Wolf told him. "All right," he conceded, "you'll present me to Rolissa Highsmith no later than tomorrow afternoon."

"There's one other small matter," Lord Brandon said.

George nodded. "No murders," he stipulated.

"There's something else I neglected to mention in my recital of my adventures as Wolf Clinton," Lord Brandon said. "It's not of the first importance; surely we can overcome it. Yet the problem must be dealt with."

"And what is it?" Wolf asked.

"Unfortunately, Rolissa might not take kindly to your being a married man."

"Never been married in my life. You don't know what you're talking about."

"Ah, but the fact is I do know. You're married and your wife, who's quite mad, resides in Canada. Her name is Alfaretta. Before we proceed any farther, we have to decide what to do with Alfaretta."

"You were the only person I could turn to," Rolissa told Marianne three weeks later as they sat side by side on the confidante in the Hilton library. "My mother won't listen to a word I say, and there's no one else. And, besides, you know him. At the musical evening, I even suspected you might favor him, but after talking to Wolf I realize you don't. He acts as if he hardly knows you."

"How did you happen to meet him?" Marianne asked. "I don't mean at the musicale, later."

"It was the strangest thing," Rolissa said. "Lord Brandon and Georgie Stansbury presented him to me almost as though I'd never met him before."

"Lord Brandon accompanied Mr. Clinton? You saw the two of them together?"

"Oh, yes, all three of them came to call on me."

Marianne nodded. That settled the matter; there *was* a real Wolf Clinton. Probably his reappearance in London had forced Lord Brandon to abandon his impersonation. She smiled to herself. Lord Brandon must be doing his utmost to prevent her from meeting the real Wolf and learning the truth.

"I know you must remember the winter of the Great Frost when the Thames froze over," Rolissa was saying. "The year they built the bonfires on the ice for the Frost Fair, the year of the terrible fogs and snowstorms when noon seemed as dark as midnight. Before I met Wolf, that's the way I was, cold and dark and drear. Nothing seemed real; it was as though I acted a part, one I didn't particularly care for. Wolf's coming has been like a thousand springtimes blossoming at once. I want to be with him constantly, and when I can't be, I want to talk about him. That's one of the reasons I came to you, Marianne, because you know him."

"Not at all well, I'm afraid." She paused, choosing her words carefully. "The Wolf Clinton you know and the one I knew a few weeks ago are two different people."

"It's odd you should put it like that," Rolissa said. "When I saw him at the musicale, my heart gave a great leap, and yet when he kissed me later that evening—do you think the less of me for letting him kiss me?—I can't say I felt anything special. But now he's completely changed. Does all this make sense to you?"

"Yes," Marianne said, "it does. And you were right in coming to me for help. I'll do whatever I can for you and Wolf." *And,* she thought, *if I can repay Lord Brandon for his cruelty at the same time, I'll do that, too. Kissing Rolissa at the musicale, indeed!* Remembering Lord Brandon's fervent courting of her during the last three weeks caused her a momentary pang. He did seem to mean what he said. But how could she trust such a deceiver? All she had to do was recall his masquerade to restoke her anger.

"I believe Wolf mentioned to me that he was married," Marianne said.

"Such an unsettling turn of events. His wife, her name was Alfaretta, died last year, and Wolf only found out a few weeks ago because the message was misdirected to somewhere in India. When I met him the second time, when he came with Lord Brandon, he was wearing a black band around his sleeve. Such a tragedy."

Alfaretta's death must be another one of Lord Brandon's inventive ideas, Marianne decided. He was a master at bringing people to life and then killing them off without a qualm.

"I'm so afraid," Rolissa said. "My mother and father absolutely forbid me to see Wolf even though they hardly know him. Not because he's been married, it's his former trade that disturbs them. He's a mere furrier, a purveyor of animal skins, my father says. Not that I care a farthing what they think of Wolf, I'll see him regardless. I'm not afraid because of what they may do but because of what *he* may do."

"Wolf you mean? What Wolf might do?"

"Exactly." Rolissa lowered her voice. "He intends to spirit me off to Gretna Green. We'll elope to Scotland. Isn't that romantic?"

Marianne was becoming confused as to what Rolissa did or did not want. "Then, eloping to Scotland isn't what you fear?"

"No, I want to elope. Did I tell you, besides all else, Wolf's a student of mathematics and I've been interested in mathematics since I was a little girl? It's as though we've lived all of our lives until now just waiting to meet, as though we were always intended for each other."

"Perhaps you were; fate can be both kind and cruel. I only wish—" Marianne broke off, not sure what she meant to say. That she wished she and Lord Brandon had been intended for one another? Instead of being doomed to go through life as antagonists? She was happy for Rolissa, yet concerned as well, for the girl seemed rash and impetuous.

"The reason I came to you," Rolissa confided, "is I'm worried because Wolf is so independent, so devil-may-care. He fears no one, not my father, not my mother, no one at all."

"I can think of worse traits in a man."

"Yet he acts as if he's still living in the wilds of Canada where men settle their quarrels with guns, knives, and fists. I'm not of age, and my father is within his legal right to forbid me to marry. And he does forbid it, so if Wolf and I try to elope to Gretna Green, he'll do his best to stop us. By force if need be."

At last the reason for Rolissa's fear became clear to Marianne. "And you're afraid Wolf will kill anyone who tries to stop your elopement."

"Exactly, isn't that what I said? I want to marry Wolf and be his wife, not spend years waiting for him to be released from prison. Or watching him hang from a gibbet."

Marianne shuddered at the image. "That would never do! But why should such a horror have to come to pass. If we apply our minds to the problem, there must be a way we can outwit your father while placating Wolf Clinton." *Just as Lord Brandon managed to deceive me,* she thought. *This, though, is different; this is an urgent cause, a matter of life or death.* "We two are certainly the equal of both your father and Wolf if we put our thinking caps on. Of course, we may need help, a man to do the yeoman work for us."

"Lord Brandon?"

Marianne hastily shook her head. "No, no, not Lord Brandon, he's fully occupied preparing for his balloon ascension. Someone else."

It was at this moment that Lucinda, hearing their voices, paused outside the library doorway where she was visible to neither Rolissa nor Marianne.

Rolissa had a sudden inspiration. "Georgie Stansbury," she cried.

"Georgie! I would never have thought of him. Because of Lucinda, I suppose."

"Georgie will do whatever I want him to do," Rolissa insisted. "Even if it means traveling farther than from here to the Scottish border."

Lucinda, realizing she was inadvertantly overhearing a private conversation, turned and hurried away. Perplexed, she pondered their words. How was Georgie involved with Rolissa? Rolissa of all people! And how did Scotland enter into it?

While Lucinda, on the way to her room, was becoming ever more alarmed as she dissected each nuance of the conversation for its meaning, Rolissa was saying, "Of course, we must keep this a secret from everyone."

"I won't tell a soul," Marianne promised, "not even Lucinda. When does Wolf plan your elopement?"

"Early on the morning after the ball. The very same morning Lord Brandon makes his balloon ascension with that Frenchman. Wolf reasons everyone will either be exhausted, have the megrims, or else be at Tattersall's to watch the flight, so they'll pay us little heed. As far as my father's concerned, Wolf is mistaken."

"I have a tiny seedling of an idea," Marianne said. "If you're able to escape London in secret, do you expect to be waylaid on the road to Gretna Green by your father and his men?"

"Yes, both Wolf and I think that's what my father has in mind. Wolf carries a brace of pistols, and he's vowed to fight his way to Scotland if he must."

"We'll have to make certain that's not necessary." If she could help Rolissa, Marianne told herself, and at the same time have her revenge on Lord Brandon, her cup would run over. What did it matter if the brew was exceedingly bitter?

"The fountain is still silent," Lord Brandon said.

"It was working for a while yesterday," Marianne told him, "but it's stopped again. Even now Mr. Stoddard and his men are on the roof repairing the pipes."

"The poor goldfish seem slow and lethargic, just the opposite of the way I feel. Think of it, Marianne, tomorrow I ascend into the sky with M. Delacroix. I'll fly over London, enjoying a view only a very few have ever been privileged to see."

"I envy you."

And she did. His excitement communicated

itself to her and mingled with her own anticipation of what the following day would bring, not only for him, but for her as well. That explained her heightened sense of awareness, Marianne assured herself, and caused the quickened beat of her heart, not Lord Brandon's nearness, not the look of passion in his eyes.

"I should be at the launching site now, but I stole a few moments to be with you." His gaze lingered on her gown. "That shade of blue," he said, "it's perfect, the color of your eyes and the color of the heavens we seek to conquer. It's a good omen."

However she felt about him, she did want the ascension to be a success. "All is in readiness?" she asked.

"At midnight we begin filling the balloon with hydrogen gas," he told her, "and continue the inflation until the early morning hours. If this good weather holds, M. Delacroix and I set sail at eleven. I hope you're at Tatt's well before that time in the event we have to ascend early."

"Would I miss seeing your conquest of the heavens?"

In truth, she regretted having to, she admitted to herself as she strolled beside him around the circle of the foyer, glancing from the corner of her eye to judge how he received her comment. He merely nodded. Good, he suspected nothing, and why should he? How could he possibly guess that at eleven on the following morning she expected to be riding north from London on the road to Gretna Green?

"Afte the flight is over," Lord Brandon said, "and as soon as we've deciphered our scientific data, I'm off to Scarborough Hall for six or seven weeks. At first I intended to delve directly into the accounts with my manager until the discrepancies were explained to my satisfaction. Now I have a scheme in mind that will see me arriving at the Hall incognito. I've spent so little time there; it's unlikely I'll be recognized."

So Lord Brandon still preferred the devious to the straightforward. It was on the tip of her tongue to make a tart remark to that effect, but she remembered in time she mustn't arouse his suspicions. All she said was "You seem genuinely interested in the affairs of your estate."

"I am, I truly am. Just as when I was a boy and I didn't rest until Frederic Ramsden and I solved the Litchfield labyrinth. I find the workings of the Hall a puzzle that invites unraveling."

At least he'd changed in some ways, Marianne told herself. Too late, too late. But was it? For an instant she regretted the plan she and Rolissa had devised, the plan they would set into motion early the next morning. Yet there could be no turning back, not now. It *was* too late.

"While I'm at the Hall poring over my accounts," Lord Brandon said, "why don't you spend a month or two traveling? London becomes unbearable in July and August. Besides, no one is left in town."

Unbearable for you, perhaps, with Wolf Clinton and myself in London while you're away and unable to prevent our meeting. To solve his problem, he meant to encourage her to travel. Another of his stratagems! How weak she'd been a moment before when she had doubted the wisdom of what she intended to do. No humiliation would be too great for Lord Brandon.

"You'd enjoy the south of France," Lord Brandon said. "A villa on the Mediterranean, perhaps, or a chalet in the Alps, depending on your taste."

She smiled thinly. "I visited Paris and the south last year, as soon as France was safe for English visitors."

"Somewhere closer to London, then? Bath has its charms at this time of year."

"Aren't you fearful that if I journey to Bath I might learn of your doings while you were there last month?" she asked teasingly.

"There's always Brighton," Lord Brandon hastened to say. "The piers, the beaches, the Regent's Palace with its Oriental domes and Chinese furnishings."

Marianne raised her eyebrows. "Brighton? Everyone visits Brighton these days. If I left London, I'd want to travel to some remote spot, a wild and lonely place of crags and sea and wind. In fact, I've been considering a trip to Scotland."

"Scotland? Why on earth would anyone want to visit Scotland?"

"For reasons of the heart, of course. What could be more romantic than Scotland with its moors, its lochs, its castles?"

"My God, even the Scots can't abide Scotland. All those Scots fortunate enough to have the money for passage are on their way to America. Soon the country will be inhabited only by sheep."

"Perhaps, then, this is the time to go, while there are still vestiges of civilization."

"You don't treat my suggestions seriously," Lord Brandon said. "I suppose you're telling me you want to stay in London for the summer." He sighed and shrugged. "Very well, I'll make haste to return from the Hall because when I do I intend to ask you a question I asked once before. Only this time I hope and pray the answer will be different."

She turned her head so as not to have to see the hope in his eyes. "I have a confession to make." She spoke rapidly to quell her rush of sympathy for him. "When you were in Bath I met a gentleman at Litchfield Hall. A certain Mr. Wolfson Clinton."

"I think I've heard the name," Lord Brandon admitted. "I believe Georgie has spoken of him."

"I'm sure he has." Marianne walked slowly ahead of him around the silent fountain.

Lord Brandon followed close behind. "Is that the entirety of your confession?" he asked.

"No, there's more and worse. I let him kiss me. I admit I shouldn't have, but I did." And the room had whirled, she remembered. Would that ever happen to her again?

"And where is this Wolf Clinton now?" Lord Brandon asked.

"On his way to Canada, I expect. He told me that was his plan, and I never had reason to doubt his word."

Lord Brandon took her by the arm and turned

her to face him. "Then, I think we can forget about him. Don't you agree?"

Looking into his blue eyes, held in thrall by the ardor of his gaze, she softened toward him.

With a rumble followed by a gurgle and a hiss, the fountain above their heads sprang to life. Water spouted high into the air, arced in graceful symmetry, fell in a silvery shower into the basins and cascaded to the pool. An unexpected new beginning, a moment touched by magic.

Lord Brandon drew her to him and kissed her, his lips insistent, his body ardent against hers. The room whirled.

After a timeless moment, she reluctantly drew away. Too late, Lord Brandon, she thought, too late. Her letter to him was already written and sealed, Georgie waited for word from her, Rolissa depended on her, and she couldn't afford to be diverted. She refused to give Lord Brandon the opportunity to deceive her once more.

And the fountain seemed to whisper, "Too late, Marianne, too late."

Chapter Fifteen

After a night of fitful sleep, Marianne rose at the sound of the church bells tolling three. She dressed with deliberate haste in the clothes she had hung at the front of her wardrobe the night before, a cream batiste gown with a single frill at the hemline, cream-colored gloves, a rose-patterned poke that concealed almost all of her black hair, and cream kid slippers. She draped a fringed pongee shawl about her shoulders.

Descending the sweep of the stairs with the town house hushed around her, she slipped from the front door and hurried down the steps to the walkway. The warm night was star-brilliant; the branches of the trees in the center of the square whispered in the breeze from the south.

She saw the phaeton at once, a dark silhouette standing several hundred paces to her right. Marianne hastened toward the carriage, but when she realized there was no one in the driver's seat, she slowed, suddenly wary. A figure stepped from the shadows, raising his top hat and bowing.

"Georgie," she said, "you startled me."

"Sorry, didn't mean to."

He helped her into the carriage, climbed up to sit beside her, flicked the reins and they were on their way.

"Actually, it's red," George said.

She pondered his remark for a moment, then smiled in understanding. "Your new phaeton," she said. "It does look almost black at night."

Black, she thought, as black and drear as her mood. The streets were no better, quiet and deserted, the houses shadowed. Lonely houses on lonely streets in an unfriendly, uncaring city. The clatter of the phaeton's metal wheels on the cobbles seemed to warn her: You can't turn back, you can't turn back. Marianne suppressed the sob that rose in her throat.

"Looks like a foreign country," George said in astonishment. "London in the early morning. I've been up and about at this time of night but always on my way home. Not at all the same as starting out."

If only she could start out fresh, Marianne thought, how differently she would direct her life, but it was too late. All she could do now was to help another find happiness.

"Turn here," she told George.

Slowing the horses, he swung the phaeton into an alleyway running behind the mansions facing on Piccadilly. "All look alike in the dark," he said. "Be lucky to find the right one."

"Stop just ahead," she told him, "where the

224

white cloth hangs over the brick wall. That's the Highsmith's."

"Ah, I smell the roses in the garden." George reined the horses to a walk and then stopped them. "By Jove," he said, "isn't that a girl sitting on the wall?"

"Of course, it's Rolissa, waiting for us. Help her down, Georgie."

"Pleasure." He leaped to the ground, walked to the wall and held up his arms. When Rolissa pushed herself off the top of the wall, he grasped her about the waist and swung her to the ground.

"Were you seen?" Marianne asked after Rolissa climbed to sit beside her in the phaeton.

"I don't think so, but I can't be certain."

"Lilies of the alley," George said as he urged the horses from the alleyway.

"I wore the perfume for you, Georgie," Rolissa told him, "because I know it's your favorite. It was the least I could do, since I'm so beholden to you." She sighed admiringly. "You're so brave to help me."

George shifted uncomfortably. "Always glad to help a lady in distress," he said. As they neared the first intersection he asked, "Where shall I drive?"

"To the new Regent Street," Rolissa told him. She glanced behind the phaeton but saw only the deserted roadway.

"Quite a coincidence," George said, glancing from one rose-patterned bonnet to the other. "Don't mind admitting you both surprised me. You and Marianne, dressed like two peas in a pod. Could be twins."

"It's not a coincidence at all," Marianne told him. "We did it on purpose."

When she didn't elaborate, George nodded. "I understand, a secret. At least you can tell me where I'm driving you this morning. Only to Regent Street?"

"We'd like you to take us at least as far as Litchfield Hall," Marianne told him.

"Litchfield Hall! But-but-but," he stammered. "Dash it all, Brandon's balloon ascends at eleven. I promised Lucy I'd escort her to Tatt's."

"You'll be back in London with time to spare," Rolissa promised. "I'm certain you will be, Georgie."

"Might be, might not be, can't be sure. Driving's slow at night. Easy to lose your way."

"This is terribly important to Rolissa," Marianne said. "And to me as well. I know you're not going to disappoint us, Georgie. We're both depending on you."

"Glad to help. Have to write a note to Lucy, though. My rooms are on the way to Regent Street. Only take me a few minutes."

Once more Rolissa glanced apprehensively behind them. "No one's following us," she said. "At least I don't see anyone."

George turned to the right and, in the middle of a long row of houses, stopped the phaeton. "Not safe on the street," he said, looping the reins to a hitching ring. "Come in, come in, I'll be done in a thrice."

He shepherded Marianne and Rolissa into the house, through a hallway and parlor into a study.

After lighting a lamp, he yanked on the maroon bellcord. "Hate to rouse Chauncey at this time of night," he said. "Can't be helped."

George sat at a desk, dipped a quill in an ink bottle and started to write. "'Unexpected engagement,'" he quoted when he'd finished. "'Unavoidable delay. Please forgive me.' Does that give her the gist of the matter?" he asked.

"It should satisfy Lucinda," Marianne said.

Rolissa was pacing in front of the hearth, now and again glancing restively at George as he folded and sealed the note. "I don't think anyone heard me slip from the house," she said. "I don't think we were followed."

"Let me look from the parlor windows to make sure," Marianne said to relieve Rolissa's anxiety.

A few moments after Marianne left the study, Chauncey, a gangling youth, his red hair tousled from sleep, entered the room from the rear of the house. When George, handing him the note, said, "For Miss Beattie," the boy nodded as though accustomed to delivering messages to Lucinda.

"Georgie," Rolissa said, "how can I ever thank you for so inconveniencing yourself."

"Not necessary, not at all."

Rolissa went to him, stood on tiptoes and kissed him on the cheek. George reddened. Seeing Chauncey standing in the rear doorway grinning at his discomfiture, he reddened still more. "Be off with you," he said sheepishly, his words sending Chauncey, still grinning, hurrying from the room.

George and Rolissa returned to the entry hall, where Marianne joined them. "There's no sign of any other carriages in the street," she said.

"We must hurry," Rolissa said as she led the way from the house. "Wolf will be waiting for us." She touched Marianne's arm. "I only wish I could see Wolf's face when he realizes what we've done."

Lucinda, like Marianne, had slept poorly but for very different reasons. She was elated and at the same time worried. Unexpected success was hers, yet an equally unforeseen disaster threatened.

The evening before, Mr. Trotter himself, Mr. Benjamin R. Trotter, proprietor of Trotter and Sons, Publishers, had called on her. "Most unfortunate," he said, "the whole mishmash is a great embarrassment to myself and to my sons as well. A new editor confused you with a lady from Liverpool who has the same given name. He intended to regretfully decline to publish her manuscript, and instead he refused yours. You can be confident we'll make amends to you for any inconvenience he may have caused."

Yet her literary success would be as nothing if she lost the affections of George Stansbury. What had she done wrong? Had she, by expecting too much too soon from Georgie, driven him into the arms of Rolissa Highsmith? Rolissa! She pursed her lips. What did Georgie see in Rolissa? Didn't he realize she was naught but an empty-headed coquette?

Lucinda left her troubled bed at half past three in the morning after being awakened by sounds in the house. Going to her window, she was in time to watch a phaeton carrying two night-dark figures drive from the square.

A few minutes later she found a letter that had been pushed under her bedroom door along with a note from Marianne asking her to deliver the message to Lord Brandon before his balloon ascension. Puzzled, she looked in Marianne's room and found her gone. Perplexed and worried, at the same time excited by the prospect of cataclysmic events, yet fearful what those events might portend, she made her way downstairs to the library, hoping to find solace, as she often did in times of trouble, in the pages of a well-loved book.

The library was warm and stuffy, so she opened the window overlooking the square before going to the bookshelves. Could Marianne's early morning departure be the result of the overheard conversation with Rolissa? Was Georgie involved in some way? Panic fluttered within her, and she hesitated in front of the bookshelves. She should do something. But what?

She heard footsteps outside the house, first approaching along the walk, then climbing to the porch. A pause ensued and then more steps, departing now. When Lucinda looked from the window, she saw a familiar figure passing beneath the street lamp.

"Chauncey," she called. "Is that you?"

George's footman stopped. "Yes, mum," he said as though regretting the admission.

"What on earth are you doing here at this time of night?" she asked. An ill-defined and irrational fear gripped her. Dark and mysterious forces were at work. Catastrophe threatened. Georgie, suddenly and desperately ill, was calling her to his bedside.

"Left you a note, mum," Chauncey said. "From the master." In the past she'd smiled when she heard Chauncey refer to Georgie as master, but now she shivered with apprehension.

"Slipped it under your door, I did," he added.

"Is Mr. Stansbury all right?"

"In fine fettle, last I seen him. Less than an hour ago, it was."

"Your master was up and about early. He must be all agog over the prospect of witnessing Lord Brandon's balloon ascension."

"Don't rightly know what roused the master so early. He was with a young lady, last I seen him."

Lucinda's eyes opened wide in astonishment. "A young lady? At four o'clock in the morning?"

Chauncey fidgeted. "Miss Highsmith it was."

Lucinda's sense of the impropriety of prying information from a servant vied with her desire to find out what brought Georgie and Rolissa together at this time of night. Curiosity triumphed by a comfortable margin. "What were they doing, Chauncey?" she asked. When the footman hesitated, she promised, "Whatever you tell me will go no farther."

"She was kissing him, seemed to me like."

Lucinda moaned. George couldn't have hurt her more if he had thrust a dagger into her heart. She staggered back from the window, Chauncey forgotten. Her breath came in short sharp gasps, her heart thudded in her chest, and she feared she was about to swoon. Clutching the edge of the writing table with both hands, she steadied herself, trying to regain some semblance of composure.

Her thoughts whirled inchoately. She took a few uncertain steps, unaware of where she was or what she was doing. Her hand touched, in turn, the base of the lamp on the table, the cover of a book, a bottle of ink. All at once she remembered the letter, Georgie's letter.

Rushing to the entry, she plucked the letter from the floor, tore open the seal and read Georgie's scrawled note: "Unexpected engagement. Unavoidable delay. Please forgive me." What did he mean by "engagement"? Where was he going at this early hour? What was he about to do that required her forgiveness?

With a groan she recalled the conversation between Marianne and Rolissa. Scotland. Gretna Green. Now she understood the awful import of their words. Georgie and Rolissa were eloping to Scotland with Marianne's help.

She crumpled the letter in her hand. With her world reduced to flinders around her, she fled up the stairs, almost colliding with Mrs. Featheringill in the hall.

"My dear Lucinda," Mrs. Featheringill said, "whatever is the matter?"

When Lucinda burst into tears, Mrs. Featheringill held out her arms, and Lucinda clung to the older woman, sobbing.

"Tell me all about it, my dear," Mrs. Featheringill said soothingly.

Between sobs, Lucinda told of the overheard

conversation, Chauncey's dark-of-the-night mission, Georgie's letter, everything. By the time she finished, she'd stopped crying.

"I don't believe George Stansbury would do such a thing," Mrs. Featheringill said firmly. "I know him and his father, and I knew his grandfather as well. Honorable men, one and all. George might act foolishly on occasion, but he's young and comes from a long line of late bloomers. He'd never be one to ride off to Scotland like a thief in the night with Rolissa Highsmith or anyone else."

"He wouldn't?" Hope enlivened Lucinda's voice.

"Of course he wouldn't." Mrs. Featheringill held Lucinda away from her. "Now here's what we'll do. You wash your face and get dressed while I wake Brabson and have him bring the curricle around to the front, and we'll get to the bottom of this jumble. Lord Brandon. Yes, he may very well hold the key, so we'll deliver Marianne's letter to him as soon as we can. Perhaps the contents will give us a clue or perhaps Lord Brandon will know what George Stansbury is up to. They're best friends, after all."

"You'll come with me?" Lucinda asked.

"Of course I will; I wouldn't miss it for the world. I've listened to snippets of talk from this one and that one for the last two months without quite knowing what mischief was afoot. Now I do believe I'm about to find out. Come with you? Just you try and stop me."

Within thirty minutes they were on their way to Tattersall's, Lucinda wearing white lawn trimmed with violet ribbon, Mrs. Featheringill a long-sleeved, black silk moire gown with a bell skirt fashionable twenty years before, an organdy fichu crossed over her chest.

By the time they arrived, the sky in the east was starting to lighten, so they were able to see the huge balloon hovering over the stable roofs. Leaving their carriage, they hurried to the roped-off exercise oval where men labored by lantern light, producing the hydrogen gas and funneling it into the envelope of the Phaeton. The balloon's basket rested on the ground, kept earthbound by stout ropes.

When they found Lord Brandon directing the inflating of the balloon, he stared in surprise at the two women but said nothing, not even when Lucinda handed him Marianne's letter. Opening the letter, he held it up to catch the light, reading swiftly. When he finished, his arm dropped lifelessly to his side while he stared straight ahead, unseeing.

Unable to restrain her curiosity, Lucinda asked, "What does Marianne say?"

"That she's on her way to Gretna Green with Mr. Wolf Clinton," he answered, his voice a monotone. Lord Brandon stuffed the letter into the pocket of his frock coat. "She must think he's me." His voice rose in indignation. "She thinks she's eloping with me when it's really Clinton. That scoundrel! Making me believe he'd lost his heart to Rolissa when actually it was Marianne he coveted. How dare he deceive her? How dare he deceive *me*?"

"Has Lord Brandon taken leave of his senses?"

Lucinda asked in an aside to Mrs. Featheringill. "I can't fathom what he's trying to say."

"No, he's not lost his reason. I'll try to explain the whole muddle to you later." Mrs. Featheringill turned to Lord Brandon. "Does Marianne say in so many words she intends to marry Mr. Clinton?" she asked.

"No, yet her meaning's clear enough. The poor girl's blameless; the fault's entirely mine. I should never have deceived her. I played a fool's game, and now it's too late to make amends."

"Do you know George's whereabouts?" Mrs. Featheringill asked. "We have reason to believe he's with Rolissa Highsmith."

"I haven't the faintest notion. I expected him to be here later this morning to watch the baloon ascension."

"A double wedding in Gretna Green," Lucinda said suddenly, "that's their plan; it's as clear as day. Marianne and Wolf, Rolissa and Georgie."

"Perhaps it's not too late to act, Lord Brandon," Mrs. Featheringill looked up at the red and gold balloon tugging at its mooring ropes. "The wind is from the south, isn't it?"

Lord Brandon wet his index finger and held it aloft. "From the southeast and fairly strong." He nodded. "You're right, Mrs. F., we do have a chance to intercept them. The odds stand ten to one against us, yet there *is* a chance. If I waste no time, I may overtake them yet." He strode to the basket, climbed a few rungs of the boarding ladder and vaulted inside.

Lucinda followed him and began to climb aboard.

"No," Lord Brandon told her, "it's much too dangerous. I'm hardly an experienced aeronaut, you know."

"Whatever you set your mind to, you do well, Lord Brandon." Lucinda clambered into the basket. "A writer doesn't only write," she said. "She must live life to the fullest as well."

Mrs. Featheringill put her foot on the bottom rung of the ladder. "Nor shall you leave without me," she told Lord Brandon. "I've always wanted to fly in a balloon, and at my age who can say if I'll ever have another chance?"

"Oh, God, women," Lord Brandon moaned. "All right," he said, reaching down and lifting Mrs. Featheringill over the basket's rim, "I've no time to waste in debate."

He called to the men working at the hydrogen generator. "Disconnect the tubes," he ordered. "Pariot, Rugh, Roemerman, Schloemer, take hold of the tether ropes, we're going aloft at once."

"But what of M. Delacroix?" one of the men wanted to know.

"To hell with M. Delacroix. I'll deal with him when the time comes. Do as I say."

In a few minutes the balloon, straining against the tether ropes, began to rise in a series of starts and stops. As soon as the basket was higher than the stable roofs, Lord Brandon leaned over the side. "Release all ropes," he said, and they sailed free.

"There's a gentleman in a blue coat running back and forth on the ground waving his arms," Lucinda said. "Now he's shaking his fist at us."

"That's M. Delacroix." Lord Brandon sighed.

"May he some day find it in his heart to forgive me."

"See what I've discovered in this box," Mrs. Featheringill said. "Flags." She held up a Tricolor and Union Jack.

"All balloons carry flags," Lord Brandon told her. "They're to be waved as we ascend. I'm not sure exactly why. To show our elation at our conquest of the elements, I expect."

Mrs. Featheringill went to the side of the basket and waved the two flags.

"Such a strange sensation," Lucinda said. "We seem to be standing still while the ground falls away below us. And up here the sun is above the horizon, yet all of London is still shrouded in darkness."

"I can see the dome of St. Paul's," Mrs. Featheringill cried, "and the Tower and the Thames cut into small pieces by its bridges. God's view of London must be akin to this."

Lord Brandon turned his back to the rising sun to gaze across the sprawl of the northern environs of the city toward the dark wooded hills along the route to Scotland. Somewhere far ahead and far below them, Wolf Clinton and Marianne drove north by northwest on their way to Gretna Green. Lord Brandon wondered how far ahead Marianne was by now, what she was doing, what she was thinking. . . .

Wolf paid the toll and waited impatiently for the keeper to open the gate. The journey on the dark and unfamiliar road had been slow, but now, with the sun rising, he was determined to make up for time lost. A glance into the shadowy interior of the barouche told him that Rolissa, covered by her silk shawl, was still sleeping.

As the gate swung to one side, a horseman rode from behind the tollhouse and galloped along the road ahead of him. Wolf was certain the rider was the same squat man he'd noticed a short time before peering from the darkness at the barouche.

He smiled grimly. He'd been wondering when Kier-Windom's hirelings would make their appearance, and now, in all probability, one of them had. Taking his two loaded and primed pistols from the seat beside him, he thrust them under his belt, allowing his coat to fall into place over them. Let Kier-Windom's men do their damnedest; he was ready.

Wolf drove away from the tollgate with the sun sending long shadows onto the road ahead of the carriage. The barouche passed through a village, rattled across a bridge, overtook a farmer's wagon, then climbed a long hill, the carriage slowing as the horses strained to conquer the grade. As they crested the hill, he saw that the road curved to the left into a woods.

A trunk of a tree blocked the road at the beginning of the turn, and though he couldn't be certain, Wolf thought he detected movement in the brush at the side of the road. He reined to a halt and waited calmly, his hands poised a few inches from his pistols.

Two roughly dressed men emerged from the

brush, one, the squat man from the tollhouse, carrying a large old-fashioned pistol. Wolf smiled when he saw the weapon. The pistol had an effective range of less than ten feet; he'd wager his life on it. Perhaps he'd have to.

"You Wolfson Clinton?" the squat man asked while his companion circled to the other side of the carriage.

"I am," Wolf replied.

"His lordship sent us to bring his daughter home. Tell her to get out of the carriage."

"She's no concern of yours." Wolf's hand slid beneath his coat and closed on the grip of one of the pistols.

The door of the barouche swung open, and the lone passenger stepped to the dirt road. A shawl covered her shoulders, but she no longer wore her bonnet. The squat man stared at her black curls in confusion.

"I'm Miss Marianne Hilton," she told him, "and there's no one else in the carriage. You're welcome to look for yourself."

Wolf, his hand still on the pistol, was startled into inaction. Where the devil was Rolissa? Where had this woman come from? Had lack of sleep deranged him?

The squat man's companion appeared from behind the carriage. "She's right," he said. "No one's inside, and the boot's full of baggage."

The squat man stepped back, mumbling incoherent words as he touched his free hand to his cap in a gesture of appeasement.

"Get that tree off the road," Wolf ordered.

As the two men dragged the tree to one side, Marianne climbed up to join Wolf on the driver's seat. When they were under way once more, Wolf demanded, "Where the hell is she?"

"Rolissa's perfectly safe. She's riding with George Stansbury on another road. They'll meet us at Litchfield Hall."

"Litchfield Hall, always Litchfield Hall." Wolf shook his head as though to clear it. "But I saw Rolissa get into this carriage on Regent Street. Not you, her. I spoke to her."

"When Rolissa entered the carriage in the dark of night, she left at once by the other door, and I took her place. She was afraid, and quite rightly so"—Marianne nodded at his pistol—"of what you might do if her father's men intercepted you on the road to Gretna Green."

"Damme!" Wolf his his knee with his fist in anger, then laughed. "I admire a girl with spirit," he said. "Litchfield Hall? That can't be far from here." He cracked the whip. "We'll be at the Hall in no time at all."

The balloon sailed steadily and gracefully northwestward, propelled by a strong southerly wind. The sun was up, and their undulating shadow preceded them across the rolling hills and valleys.

"I see a red phaeton," Lucinda said, pointing down and ahead.

Lord Brandon removed a spyglass from its wooden case, extended the glass and peered through its magnifying lenses. "It's Georgie's new phaeton, right enough. And Rolissa's sitting beside him."

"I knew it," Lucinda cried. "They *are* eloping. My worst fears are—"

"If we've learned one truth from this muddle," Mrs. Featheringill interrupted, "it's that things are not always what they appear."

"Georgie's following a most peculiar route," Lord Brandon said. "He's on the old road to Litchfield Hall." He raised the spyglass slightly until he focused on the new road. "There's a barouche hellbent in the same direction." He cursed under his breath. "Wolf Clinton's at the reins, and Marianne's with him."

"I see them now," Lucinda said. "Aren't they almost to Tart's Turn?"

"They are. That fool Canadian will never negotiate the Turn at that speed." Lord Brandon reached above him and pulled a rope to release hydrogen from the top of the balloon's envelope. "I'm bringing us down," he announced.

The balloon lurched and then began a rapid descent. . . .

In the phaeton, George glanced skyward. "Good God! Lord Brandon. And Lucinda! What in the name of heaven is she doing up there?"

Rolissa cried out in alarm. "Their balloon's falling from the sky!"

*　　*　　*

In the plummeting balloon, Lord Brandon stared down at Wolf Clinton's barouche. "They've come to the Turn," he said. "Slow down, Clinton, you fool, slow down! My God, the carriage is overturning; it's on its side. They'll all be killed."

"Brandon!" Lucinda grasped his arm. "Those trees. We're about to hit those trees!"

Chapter Sixteen

Lord Brandon dropped a bag of sand from the basket, and the balloon's rate of descent lessened. He tossed another bag over the side and then another; the balloon, lighter now, began to rise. The basket's bottom scraped the uppermost branches of the oaks, held momentarily, then pulled free. Seeing a field beyond the trees, he released more hydrogen, and the balloon again drifted earthward.

Marianne sat up. Providentially, she had landed in thick grass when the barouche overturned and, except for a few bruises, was unhurt. The carriage lay on its side, the horses whinneying in fright as they struggled to free themselves from the harness, while Wolf Clinton sprawled, unmoving, on the grass a few feet from her.

She knelt beside him, noting with dismay his face beneath his black beard was pale and there was an angry dark bruise on his forehead. Biting her lip, she rested a tentative hand on his chest, then sighed in relief. Thank God he was breathing.

He needed help; she must find someone to see to him. And she would. But Brandon came first. The last she had seen the balloon, it was falling toward a row of oaks a short distance from the spot where the carriage overturned.

Was Brandon injured? She could do nothing else until she was assured of his safety. If anything had happened to him. . . .

Marianne stood up and looked around her. The road was deserted; the balloon nowhere in sight. Off to her left the towers of Litchfield Hall rose against the western sky. Brandon, where was Brandon? She hurried into the field toward the oaks. As she came closer, she saw the orange and crimson envelope of the balloon between the trunks of the trees.

Pushing her way through a screen of brush, she came into another field. The balloon was down, the basket sitting upright, the partly full envelope rippling in the breeze and what appeared to be an anchor tethering basket and envelope to the ground. As she started forward, Lord Brandon leaped from the basket and ran toward her. Behind him she recognized Lucinda and, remarkably, old Mrs. Featheringill clutching a small Union Jack.

Marianne stopped. Lord Brandon stopped. Her heart pounded. He was safe, safe, safe.

The hurts of the past fell away from her, the fact that he had deceived her no longer had a meaning, and her desire for revenge was gone. He was alive, and he was here; that was all that mattered. They'd been offered a new beginning; the slate had been wiped clean of misunderstandings leaving only her love for him, a love she had resisted for so long, a love grown stronger in the crucible of adversity.

She had rejected his offer months before—it seemed years—because she had thought he was like her father. How wrong she'd been! All his life her father had fled from misfortune, first journeying to the Continent and then planning to embark for America. Just as Grandfather Alder Hilton had retreated from London to Edgemoor.

Lord Brandon didn't flee from trouble; he turned and faced whatever threatened him. He stood his ground. Though she might not always approve of his methods, she couldn't fault either his courage or tenacity.

They ran to one another with open arms. He embraced her and held her close.

"Everything I did was for love of you," he said, his breath tingling in her hair.

"I know," she assured him. "I think I've always known without ever admitting the truth to myself until now. Just as you must have known I never cared a whit for Wolf; it was always you, Brandon."

He tilted her chin and kissed her, and she realized that no matter what had happened or would happen, she belonged to him and he to her. Forever.

After a while she became aware that Lucinda and Mrs. Featheringill were with them, and then she remembered Wolf. Taking Lord Brandon's hand, she led him from the field, the other two women following them. When they came to the next field, they saw George's phaeton cautiously approaching Tart's Turn. By the time they reached the barouche, George was unhitching its horses. When he finished, he and Lord Brandon carried Wolf to the phaeton.

Helped by two farmers who had witnessed the accident, they rode to the Hall. After Lord Brandon sent for a doctor, he and George carried Wolf into the drawing room and laid him on a sofa. Rolissa knelt at Wolf's side while George took Lucinda to a far corner of the room and began an involved explanation about why he had been driving Rolissa on the road to Gretna Green.

Harriet, summoned from her bedchamber by a maid, came into the drawing room in her dressing gown. "This house has seen so many tragedies," she said, looking at Wolf's unconscious form. "I pray this isn't another!"

George, having convinced Lucinda of his innocence, said, "If only my father were here; he's had medical training."

"But, as you see, I am here." The general strode into the room garbed in robe and nightcap. "Don't stare," he said, "haven't any of you ever seen a man in nightdress before?" He bent over Wolf and examined the swelling on his forehead. "Have them bring me cold compresses," he told George. "I don't believe this man's hurt too badly."

Minutes later a footman hurried into the room with a basin of water in his hands and linens draped over one arm. The general cleaned Wolf's bruise before placing a damp cloth over the swelling on his forehead.

Wolf moaned. He opened his eyes and, squinting, looked from face to face, smiling a little when he saw Rolissa.

"Thank God he's all right," Marianne murmured.

Wolf pushed himself up on one arm. He glanced at the clock on the mantel, its hands at ten minutes after ten. He pulled a watch from his pocket, frowned, held the watch to his ear, then looked at Harriet.

"Mother," he said, "that clock's either three hours fast or it's stopped."

"Mother!" Harriet stared at him, perplexed. "I'm not your mother. The accident has deranged him!" she said to the general.

Wolf touched his forehead, grimaced in pain and, for a moment, closed his eyes. When he opened them again, he sat up. "I remember it all now," he said. "Wolf Clinton. Rolissa." He took her hands and drew her up beside him on the sofa. "My dear, dear Rolissa," he said.

She put her arms around him and pressed her face against his chest.

Wolf looked once more at Harriet Ramsden. "But you *are* my mother," he said, "because I'm Frederic Ramsden. I wasn't drowned when father's canoe overturned; I was swept miles downriver where I was pulled from the water by a French-Canadian trapper. Since the capsizing, I've remembered nothing of my past until this very moment." He unbuttoned the top of his shirt and drew the garment down to reveal a crimson mark in the shape of a shield.

"The birthmark!" Lucinda cried triumphantly. "I knew all along that Wolfson Clinton was Frederic Ramsden."

Harriet ran forward to kneel beside Wolf. "You *are* my son," she cried, pressing his hand to her cheek, "you are a Ramsden!"

How Harriet has changed, Marianne thought. *She used to speak in questions; now she uses exclamations. I wonder why.*

"This will take a bit of getting used to," the general said, not seeming entirely pleased by the turn of events.

Wolf, now Frederic, glared at him. "And you, sir," Frederic said. "Although this may not be the proper time or place to inquire, still I must ask what your intentions are toward my mother."

"Strictly honorable, my boy, don't leap to wrong conclusions based on insufficient evidence. We plan to marry within the fortnight."

Wolf nodded, satisfied.

Lucinda turned to George. "You told me Wolf had no birthmark." She frowned. "I trust you," she told him, "knowing you never lie, and yet he does have a birthmark as we all can plainly see."

"Easily explained," George said. "The Wolf I examined for the birthmark was Lord Brandon while the Wolf we have here is the real Wolf who isn't the real Wolf at all but Frederic Ramsden returned, as it were, from the dead. And so, since Lord Brandon, to the best of my knowledge, has no birthmark, I couldn't find the Ramsden shield on his shoulder, now could I, Lucy?"

"I'm certain you're right, Georgie," Lucinda said in a most doubtful tone.

"Fortunately," Rolissa said, "my father and mother will now most assuredly withdraw their objections to our marriage. How could they not welcome the earl of Litchfield as a son-in-law? You will forgive them for their misguided stubbornness, won't you, Wolf? Frederic?"

"Certainly, if you wish it, my love," Frederic said. "In my own good time, however, in my own good time."

"Not only will Harriet and I wed," the general informed them, "we also intend to offer to raise Paul, since we've both taken a strong fancy to the lad. I have selfish motives as well. During the Peninsula Campaign, I came to know a captured Frenchman, a General LaMothe, who had sired four children after reaching the advanced age of forty. His offspring revivified him, he claimed, and to judge by the man's energy, they most certainly did. If Paul agrees and if neither Miss Hilton nor Frederic offers an objection, we'll bring the lad here to Litchfield Hall this very day."

"I'm positive Paul will be happy here," Marianne said.

"How could I object?" Frederic asked. "Haven't I been raised by strangers most of my life? Having enjoyed loving homes both here and in Canada, how can I deny one to another? I only hope Paul will consent as well."

That Paul Stansbury, as he became following his adoption, did consent, and came to live at Litchfield Hall, with the happiest of results for all concerned, is well known to the many lovers of music who are acquainted with the details of his long and dazzling career.

"This is remarkable," Harriet said. "In the short span of a few hours, I've found a husband and a son and perhaps a second son as well!"

"All of us being here together is even more remarkable," George said. "Yesterday I'd have given anyone at Tatt's fifty to one against."

"The actual odds," Rolissa said, "are greater than that." She glanced at Frederic. "More likely they're nine raised to the ninth power to one against."

"Even greater." Frederic removed a pencil from his pocket and began to calculate on a piece of paper. "Give me ten minutes," he said, "and I'll have an approximate answer."

The complete answer, of course, took much longer to calculate. Not until almost nine years later did Trotter and Sons publish the ground-breaking treatise, "An Introduction to the laws of Probability and Chance," a work that established the earl of Litchfield as the preeminent authority in what had become his chosen field.

"Whatever the odds," George said, "there's one matter I don't intend to leave to chance. Nevermore will I risk losing you, Lucy. Dash it all, when I saw you plummeting toward the trees in Lord Brandon's balloon, I said to Rolissa, 'If she dies, I die as well.' I want you not only as a valued friend, Lucy; I want you to be my wife. Will you do me the great honor of marrying me?"

"Oh, Georgie." She ran to him and hugged him. "I will, Georgie, I will."

"And I won't object," George declared magnanimously, his arm around her, "if, after we are man and wife, you continue writing your novels in your spare time."

"Thank you, Georgie." *Not that I had any intention of stopping,* she told herself.

"I would think all that has happened during these last few months," Marianne told Lucinda, "including your courtship and Lord Brandon's deception and Frederic's recovery of his memory, would make an exciting work of fiction."

"No villains," George objected at once. "Not unless you include those two hirelings of Rolissa's father's. A good story needs villains, you know."

"Villains aren't necessary," Mrs. Featheringill said, "not as long as we have ourselves."

"Besides no villains," George went on, "the tale's too preposterous by half. Neither Lucy nor anyone else could ever make it believeable.

But Lucinda, as we know, in this one matter at least, didn't follow the advice of her future husband, and the story, with the true identities of the characters artfully concealed, enriched English literature and, in the opin-

ion of many, established Lucinda Stans-
bury's claim to be the precursor of Charles
Dickens.

All Lucinda said at the time, however, was "I'm certain you're right, Georgie, as you always are. I should trust your judgment; I should trust you. I don't know why I ever suspected you favored Rolissa."

"No reason for you to," George assured her, "none at all."

"I knew in my heart she was only your good friend, even when I discovered she'd kissed you." As George reddened, Lucinda went on. "You didn't enjoy her kissing you, did you, Georgie?"

George met her gaze with a look of complete sincerity. "Absolutely not," he said.

Years later, during one of his famous "chats" with his friend the prime minister, those wide-ranging discussions that dramatically altered the course of the Empire, Sir George, for this occurred after he was knighted by the queen, admitted the truth. "Probably my first full-fledged lie," he said. "Dash it all, Dizzy, of course I enjoyed it. In those days Rolissa wasn't the very proper matron she is today. Always thought the lie changed me from a youth to a man. Or at least started the change. Lost some of my innocence. Not a good trade-off, perhaps, giving up innocence in the name of expediency, yet inevitable."

Lord Brandon cleared his throat. "Since this appears to be the time to make announcements of forthcoming felicitous events," he said, "I must add my own." He paused. "But first let me apologize to Marianne for deceiving her by assuming the garb and appearance of Wolf Clinton. What I did was misguided and hurtful, and I'm sincerely sorry. I've had done with deception. I've even abandoned my scheme to arrive at Scarborough Hall incognito."

"You have no need to apologize," Marianne told him. "I think that over the years, *I've* been the real impostor, since I've posed as a woman living life to the fullest while all the time refusing to commit myself to others. I've been afraid, afraid of being hurt. Only now do I realize what I've missed by trying to avoid all risk. Life itself is risk; good comes along with bad, the better with the worse. I can accept that now." She clasped Lord Brandon's hand in hers. "I can if you're at my side, Brandon."

"I will be, now and always. That's my announcement; Marianne has accepted my proposal and will become my wife."

Cries of "Hear, hear," and "Huzza," rang out.

"I'll be your wife," Marianne said, "yet I don't recall a proposal."

"My offer for your hand was made some months ago," Lord Brandon reminded her. "I've never withdrawn it, and now, at long last, you've accepted. I don't think I'm required to offer another proposal and then another, *ad infinitum.*"

Marianne smiled up at him. "Not as long as the choice of the destination of our wedding trip is mine."

"Fair enough. Where would you like to go? To France? To Bath or Brighton?" He smiled, albeit a trifle thinly. "Perhaps to Scotland?"

"No, none of those places. When you persuaded me you were Wolf Clinton, I read book after book about your supposed homeland and became intrigued. I'd like to journey to Canada and perhaps on to the United States."

"Canada? The United States?" His tone said he couldn't have been more surprised if she had proposed a balloon ascension to the moon. Finally he sighed. "A bargain's a bargain," he conceded. "If you're serious about traveling to the New World, that's where we'll go."

They did go, of course, and remained for many years in North America, where their trials and triumphs are too well-known to warrant repetition here. It must be said, however, that Alder Hilton's desire for an heir was amply fulfilled.

"Breakfast is served," the Ramsden butler announced.

"If you'll all come to the dining room," Harriet said. "Unfortunately, because of the number of guests and the shortness of time for preparation, we'll only be able to serve four courses."

As the others left the study, Marianne lingered to sit beside Mrs. Featheringill on a settee. "All of us

254

have found love," she said to the older woman. "If only there were a way you could fully share our joy."

"All my life," Mrs. Featheringill said, "I've wanted to ascend into the sky in a balloon, and now I have. If I can be an aeronaut at my age, if I can go gallivanting around the countryside, isn't every possibility under the sun open to me? All I must do now is decide what I shall try next."

"You're a marvelous woman," Marianne said. "I only hope I'll have half your enthusiasm when I'm your age."

"You will, my dear, you will." Mrs. Featheringill settled back on the settee. "What with the balloon ascension and tramping in the fields and missing my morning nap, I've grown tired. I think I'll catch forty winks before I go in to breakfast."

She closed her eyes and was asleep almost at once, a smile brightening her wrinkled face. *What can she be dreaming about?* Marianne asked herself. . . .

Mrs. Featheringill stood in the basket of a balloon rising higher and higher above Litchfield Hall, rising into the heavens toward the fiery ball of the sun. When she leaned over the rim and saw the Hall growing smaller and smaller below her, she raised the Union Jack and began to wave the flag from side to side.

Still the balloon ascended until Mrs. Featheringill, no longer old but in the bloom of her youth, spied the smudge of London to the south, Gretna

Green and all of Scotland far to the north, Wales and Ireland to the west. She peered into each and every home from the most palatial mansion to the humblest cottage—isn't everything possible when we dream?—and in not one in all of the United Kingdom did she find happier or better favored men and women than those gathered at Litchfield Hall on that July morning in the year 1817.